W9-BNL-881

Another gunshot rang out.

More glass shattered. The tension in her chest tightened as anxiety gripped her.

"Stay here," Detective James said.

Laney didn't have time to argue. He pushed away from her, his gun drawn, and approached the door.

Please don't let him get killed, she silently prayed, her palms pressed into the cool tile floor of her entryway. Shards of glass lay around her, a reminder of the gravity of the situation. Would they make it out of this alive?

The detective had been a thorn in her side, to say the least. He'd put her through the ringer at the station. Then again, she supposed he was just doing his job. But still, she didn't want to see him hurt. Especially not after he'd shown a halfway-human side of himself in the car.

"Sol, put the gun down!" Detective James yelled.

Laney sucked in a quick breath. Sol? Sol was shooting at her? Had the man lost his mind? Was this what grief did to a person?

Laney knew the answer to that question: yes.

Christy Barritt's books have won a Daphne du Maurier Award for Excellence in Suspense and Mystery and have been twice nominated for the RT Reviewers' Choice Best Book Award. She's married to her Prince Charming, a man who thinks she's hilarious—but only when she's not trying to be. Christy's a self-proclaimed klutz, an avid music lover and a road trip aficionado. For more information, visit her website at christybarritt.com.

Books by Christy Barritt

Love Inspired Suspense

Keeping Guard
The Last Target
Race Against Time
Ricochet
Desperate Measures
Hidden Agenda
Mountain Hideaway
Dark Harbor
Shadow of Suspicion

The Security Experts

Key Witness
Lifeline
High-Stakes Holiday Reunion

SHADOW OF SUSPICION

CHRISTY BARRITT

HARLEQUIN® LOVE INSPIRED® SUSPENSE

If you purchased this book without a cover you should be aware
that this book is stolen property. It was reported as "unsold and
destroyed" to the publisher, and neither the author nor the
publisher has received any payment for this "stripped book."

Recycling programs
for this product may
not exist in your area.

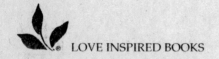 LOVE INSPIRED BOOKS

ISBN-13: 978-0-373-67804-4

Shadow of Suspicion

Copyright © 2017 by Christy Barritt

All rights reserved. Except for use in any review, the reproduction
or utilization of this work in whole or in part in any form by any
electronic, mechanical or other means, now known or hereinafter
invented, including xerography, photocopying and recording, or in
any information storage or retrieval system, is forbidden without
the written permission of the editorial office, Love Inspired Books,
195 Broadway, New York, NY 10007 U.S.A.

This is a work of fiction. Names, characters, places and incidents are
either the product of the author's imagination or are used fictitiously, and
any resemblance to actual persons, living or dead, business establishments,
events or locales is entirely coincidental.

This edition published by arrangement with Love Inspired Books.

® and TM are trademarks of Love Inspired Books, used under license.
Trademarks indicated with ® are registered in the United States Patent
and Trademark Office, the Canadian Intellectual Property Office and in
other countries.

www.Harlequin.com

Printed in U.S.A.

And what does the Lord require of you? To act justly
and to love mercy and to walk humbly with your God.
–Micah 6:8

This book is dedicated to those who put their lives
on the line in order to protect others: police, firefighters,
military and countless others. Thank you.

ONE

Laney Ryan paused, her fingers poised over her keyboard midstroke. A noise outside her suburban home caused her spine to clinch and a moment of fear to seize her thoughts.

She was being silly. The sound was probably her neighbor across the street returning home. Or maybe a deliveryman was dropping off a package. It was nothing to be concerned over.

Her instincts blazed, and she was unable to believe either of those scenarios. Something was going on outside her house—something she needed to prepare for.

Quickly, she turned off her computer and stashed it in the locked drawer hidden beneath her desk. Wasting no time, she stood. She had to get to her bedroom to grab her gun.

She'd only taken one step in that direction when her front door burst open.

A flash bang exploded in her entryway, and smoke filled the house. Feet stampeded across her floor as an unseen army invaded her space. As enemies breached her territory. As danger closed in.

She ducked by the dining room table and stifled a scream, unwilling to give away her presence even though panic rushed through her. She grabbed the edge of a chair, unable to see. Smoke blocked her vision, filled her lungs, burned her eyes.

What was going on? Had someone discovered what she did for a living? Would they try to make her talk using whatever means necessary?

Fear trembled through her bones. She'd known this day might come, but she'd hoped it wouldn't. Prayed it wouldn't.

More smoke stung her eyes. A cough caught in her throat, and she tried to hold it back. Shouts sounded around her.

How many of them were there? How many men had infiltrated her home? How long would it be before the smoke cleared and they found her?

Her house—her haven—suddenly felt like a war zone. She swallowed hard, trying to remember all the training that had been drilled into her in case she was ever captured and interrogated. Silence was of the essence. She knew secrets that could bring this country down. And in the wrong hands... She shuddered to think about what would happen.

A man in SWAT uniform appeared in front of her, his gun raised. "Laney Ryan, you're under arrest."

"For what?" she demanded.

Another cop pulled her to her feet and jerked her arms behind her with enough force to snap her bones as he pressed handcuffs around her wrists. Her body instantly ached.

"You're the prime suspect in the disappearance of Sarah Novak."

Her heart plunged. Sarah? What had happened to her sweet neighbor? The girl was only fifteen, and Laney thought the world of her.

"What's wrong with Sarah? What happened?" Her voice trembled as she braced herself for whatever news was about to come.

No one answered her. The cop behind her shoved her toward the front door as more officers invaded her home, searching every nook and cranny. Probably looking for evidence of what had happened. But why there? Why her?

Each step felt surreal, like something that happened on a TV show, but not in her real life. Panic threatened to engulf her as reality set in. She was being arrested. She had to stop this before it had a domino effect on her future.

"You've got this all wrong. I would never hurt Sarah," she rushed to tell them.

The cop behind her didn't seem to hear anything. "You have the right to remain silent. Anything you say can and will…"

The words faded as a haze came over her. Laney had just seen Sarah that morning. She and her father, Sol, had stopped by and asked for help hemming a skirt for a school event that weekend.

Sarah was only fifteen. She had so much of life ahead of her. What if she was hurt? Or worse? The thought caused Laney's heart to lurch.

Please, Father, let her be okay. Watch over her. Protect her.

A shock of cold air hit her as the cop shoved her onto the front porch. The stay-at-home mom across the street stood in her front yard, gripping her toddler's hand as she watched everything unfold with a look of horror on her face.

That wasn't even Laney's biggest concern at the moment. She couldn't care less about what her neighbors thought. Her biggest concern was Sarah.

Shouting sounded in the distance. Laney pulled her gaze toward the noise. *What now?*

Sol, she realized.

He stood on the edge of her lawn, between her house and his. His face was red with anger, and a female cop restrained him from lunging at Laney. His body language clearly screamed that he was in attack mode.

"Where's my daughter? What did you do with

her?" the slight man shouted. He looked ready to spring. "You're a monster!"

Laney's heart plunged. How could Sol think she had anything to do with this? She loved Sarah as if she were her own daughter. She would never, ever do anything to put her in jeopardy.

She opened her mouth. She wanted to say something. To convince Sol of her innocence. To explain that she had no idea where Sarah was.

But no words would leave her throat.

Poor Sarah.

Had she seemed okay that morning? No. Now that she thought about it, Sarah had seemed melancholy when she was at her house.

She'd whispered to Laney before she left, "Can we talk sometime?"

Laney had smiled and told her, "Of course." She figured it was the typical teenage problems: boys, college, grades, pimples even.

Would things be different right now if Laney had taken the time to listen to her then? But she hadn't been able to. Sarah had to go to school, Sol had been there, and Laney had to start working. She knew the dilemma would haunt her, though. The what-ifs were the worst.

She'd experienced them many times before. She'd lost sleep over questions like that. Nearly lost her mind, for that matter.

The officer shoved her into the back of a brown police sedan and slammed the door. At least the inside of the vehicle was warm, a stark contrast to the brittle winter day outside. The scent of evergreen filled the air, strangely comforting. But only for a moment.

The man in the front seat turned toward her, his eyes perceptive and hard—yet disturbingly beautiful with their crystal coloring. He was broad and imposing with light brown hair, a square jawline and a five-o'clock shadow.

"Ms. Ryan," he started. "My name is Detective Mark James. We need you to answer a few questions."

"Of course."

"What did you do with Sarah Novak?" His voice sounded all business, like he wasn't the kind of person to be messed with or questioned or who you wanted on your bad side.

"Nothing. I have no idea where Sarah is," she told him, sagging into the seat.

Laney needed to contact her boss, Nicholas Mclean. He would be able to explain who Laney was, why she was trustworthy and incapable of this. Her job with the CIA was classified, and they even used a different company name as a front.

"Don't play games, Ms. Ryan. We have a witness that proves you were the last person to be seen with Sarah. There's no need to draw this out. You'll only make this harder on yourself."

What was he talking about? That couldn't be true. Plenty of people would have seen Sarah since then. First at the bus stop. Then at school. "I'm telling you—I would never do anything to hurt Sarah. I think of her like a daughter."

He raised his chin, his gaze still assessing. "Like the daughter you always wanted? How far were you willing to take that?"

Her mouth dropped open at his implications. "What are you saying? That because I'm childless I would kidnap someone else's daughter and stow her away somewhere?"

"Yes, that's precisely what I'm saying." Those beautiful crystal eyes now looked steely blue.

She shook her head with every ounce of her strength. She had to get through to him and convince him of her innocence. "You're dead wrong. I would never do that. Never. I don't know where all of this came from, but the last time I saw Sarah, she was with her father and she was about to head to the bus stop."

"A witness places her back at your house at 11:30 this morning."

Her jaw dropped. "11:30? That's ridiculous. I wasn't even home at 11:30. I was walking around the neighborhood, getting in my exercise, just like I always do."

"Can anyone prove that?"

She let out an audible sigh, realizing the futility of her argument. "A couple of drivers passed me, but no one I know. I walk almost every day at the same time. It's part of my routine." A routine that anyone observant enough would have noticed.

Laney should have been more careful. But she'd always been a creature of routine. Routines brought her comfort, something she immensely needed in her life since the murder of her husband three years ago.

"So, no? You have no one to corroborate that?"

She nibbled on her bottom lip, the first touch of despair creeping into her psyche. This was bad. Really bad. But once the police dug deeper, certainly they would see her innocence. They'd know whoever placed Sarah at her house at eleven thirty was wrong.

"No, there's no one I know of who can verify that," she finally said. "I live alone. I'm a bit of a loner."

Why couldn't she have run into someone today of all days? Normally she'd at least catch a glimpse of a neighbor as she was out. But not today. It had been cold and overcast out, the kind of weather that kept people inside. Up until six months ago, it would have kept Laney inside also. She'd used any excuse possible. She'd been so proud of herself for stepping outside of her comfort zone, for taking baby steps toward a more normal routine and out of the isolation that had consumed her.

"Mr. Novak said you'd been arguing with him about his daughter lately."

Laney let out a little gasp. How in the world had that come up? And did the police really think it was relevant? Obviously they did since the detective had mentioned it. They thought it gave her motive.

"I just hated to see her so unhappy," Laney started, the car suddenly feeling hot and stuffy. "It wasn't my place to speak up about how Sol was raising her. I admit that. I even apologized to Sol for interfering. Sarah just looked like she needed someone to talk to."

The detective shifted, his eyes perceptive and keen as he watched her every reaction. "What didn't you agree with?"

Laney had done nothing wrong, she reminded herself. She just had to speak the truth and trust that honesty would win over the accusations against her. "Her father was so hard on her, and she's such a good girl. She was never allowed to do anything. She came home, took care of the house after school and did her schoolwork. Day after day. She had no life. No chance to hang out with friends. Sol took being overprotective to the extreme."

"I take it he didn't react well to your reprimand?"

Laney frowned. "Not at all. I apologized for interfering. I usually keep to myself. But I guess my talk did some good because Sol finally decided to let Sarah go to the school social this weekend.

I was going to be a chaperone. It was the only way he would say yes. I'd never seen Sarah look so happy."

"I see."

Laney rubbed her forehead, feeling a headache coming on. "Look, I have no idea where she went or what's going on, but I know every minute you spend focusing on me is a minute spent focusing on the wrong person."

Her words didn't seem to affect the detective. "I'll be the judge of that."

With that, the man exited the sedan, leaving Laney in the backseat feeling like she carried the weight of the world on her shoulders.

Mark James stepped from his police issued sedan and approached the head of the SWAT team, a man who also happened to be his partner. Jim Swanson stood near the porch of the stately brick home as the rest of the SWAT members filed out. A team of detectives now swarmed the inside, looking for any evidence that Laney had taken Sarah. If there was anything there, they would find it.

He mentally reviewed the time line. Sol got a call from school around twelve saying Sarah never showed up, so he'd reached out to a neighbor who said she'd seen Sarah go into Laney's at eleven thirty. Sol claimed he tried to call Laney from work, but that her line had been busy. In a panic, he'd decided to head home and check things out himself.

While in his car driving home, he'd gotten a ransom call from someone claiming to have abducted Sarah. The kidnapper wanted one-hundred thousand dollars and indicated that Sol should stay tuned for directions. Sarah had been placed on the other line as confirmation that she was alive. Before she was cut off, she'd mentioned a woman and she'd said Laney's name.

Mark could see Sol standing in his yard. The man's eyes were glazed, his shoulders hunched and his expression haggard. Two officers surrounded him, making sure he didn't do anything irrational. They were also monitoring his communications so they would know when Sarah's abductors contacted him again and hopefully be able to trace the call and find out their location.

"What do you think?" Mark asked.

Jim Swanson shrugged. "She looked shocked when we came into the house. I didn't see any guilt in her gaze. Only surprise and fear. You?"

Mark looked back at his sedan and remembered the moisture he'd seen running from Laney Ryan's eyes earlier. He'd been in this line of work for long enough to know not to let tears get to him. They could be deceitful. But, for some reason, seeing this suspect crying clutched his heart.

"The woman across the street placed Sarah here at Ms. Ryan's house before she disappeared,"

Mark said. "They say the girl went inside and never came out."

Jim shook his head. "Sarah's not in the house now. If that's true, where did she go? Where could Laney have taken her?"

"Our guys are checking out the backyard now to see if there's any evidence of a scuffle back there, right?"

"That's right. But what about motive? That's what doesn't make sense."

Mark thought about the conversation he'd had with Laney in his sedan. "It's hard to say, but she didn't sound very impressed with Sol's parenting skills. Maybe she was trying to help the girl in some kind of twisted way."

"We need to bring her in until we can thoroughly investigate," Jim said.

"I agree. I'm not sure we have enough evidence to keep her in custody, though."

"We can stall for as long as possible, until something turns up."

Mark turned back to the sedan and watched Laney for a moment. He hadn't known what he'd expected, but certainly not the beautiful woman who'd been led out in handcuffs. The petite woman had light brown hair that was cut level with her chin. She was bookish and looked smart. Her green eyes had a hint of firecracker behind them while her voice had sounded soft and kind.

None of those things meant anything, though.

The only thing that mattered was finding Sarah Novak. He wouldn't let another girl disappear forever.

Just like Lauren had.

He'd never gotten over the loss. It was one of the reasons he'd requested to be on the Missing Persons Unit here with the Richmond PD. He didn't want other people to go through what he had.

Just then, Sol began shouting into his phone from across the yard. His demeanor went from defeated to wired.

"Sarah? Is that you?" he yelled.

Mark rushed toward him. The man put his phone on Speaker, a frantic look on his face—a frantic expression Mark understood all too well. He'd lived it before.

"Dad?" The line was broken and only bits of sentences were getting through. "Help...me."

"Darling, I want to help. Where are you?"

"Dad...don't know..." Static filled the line. "But Laney..."

Sol's face turned red. "Laney what? Laney took you?"

"I'm..." Garbled words filled the silence until she ended with "Please help."

"Please, honey, can you tell me where you are? Who took you?"

"...Laney," Sarah said again.

The line went dead.

TWO

An hour later, Laney sat across from the hand-some yet cold detective at the police station. Since they'd been in the room, he'd been even-keeled—not friendly, not angry. In fact, he'd been so calm that it was almost unnerving. He had eyes that didn't easily trust. A gaze that was assessing. Body language that screamed cautious.

She might be trained as a computer program-mer, but her entire life she'd practiced reading people. She'd always preferred to stay on the fringe, in the places where she could observe and study others. Her peers had thought she was strange in high school because she'd been so quiet, but she'd always thought that she was being the person God created her to be. She'd rather be different than compromise her authenticity.

Her gaze flickered around the room now. The space reminded her of the detective: stark and neat. There was no table, nothing to use as a bar-rier to separate herself from the man across from her. There were only two chairs. The setup left her feeling exposed and vulnerable.

Laney was sure they'd planned it that way.

She was the police's number-one suspect, she realized. They weren't focusing on anyone else right now—just her.

That was a mistake.

That meant that the real person who'd abducted Sarah was getting farther and farther away. The thought made her gut turn with disgust.

Earlier, when she'd been given a phone call, she'd tried to reach Nicholas, her boss with the CIA. He hadn't answered—and he *always* answered. What did that mean?

Panic tickled her gut, her nerves, her thoughts.

At the moment, silence filled the room—probably another method of trying to get Laney to talk. It was working.

"You're focusing on the wrong person." Laney had already repeated that several times, but no one seemed to care. How could she get through to them?

"Ms. Ryan, Sarah called. She said your name." The detective leaned toward her, his gaze like a laser.

Her heart lurched. She knew how it sounded. But she also knew the truth. "She was probably calling out for my help. She trusts me. She knows I'd never hurt her."

"Which makes it even worse that you would betray her like this."

"But I didn't betray her!" Tears rushed to Laney's eyes, and she pulled her sleeve-covered hands over her face as despair bit deep.

This system seemed so messed up, and she was helpless to do anything about it. She was at the mercy of this detective. Of the justice system.

She'd just started trusting again. After her husband's murder, it had been difficult. Panic attacks had plagued her, as well as nightmares. She'd been making progress, but now this. Her therapist had his work cut out for him when all of this was over.

Detective James leaned closer and lowered his voice. "Just tell me what you did with her."

Laney closed her eyes, exhausted from repeating herself. "I'm sure witnesses told you that no one saw me leave the house with Sarah. Because I didn't leave the house with her. I don't know why she came over while I was on my walk. I don't know how she got inside or where she went from there. But I didn't do anything with her."

He sighed and leaned back as if weary from the conversation. "Anyone else have a key?"

"No."

"You sound concerned about her. Were you desperate to get her away from her father?"

Laney shook her head more adamantly. "No. Not at all. Why won't you believe me? I've been framed for this. I'm innocent here. Check my record. It's clean."

"We did check it. You're right. You have no priors. Stranger things have happened, though."

She leaned back, determined to think everything through. Something wasn't making sense to her, and she needed to pinpoint just what that was. Finally, it dawned on her. The way everything had played out today didn't make sense.

The situation had escalated too quickly. The police had just barged into her home and deemed her guilty. She realized the urgency of the matter, but something was missing.

"Don't you think sending a SWAT team to my house is a little extreme?" she started. "You could have just questioned me."

"In situations like this, time is of the essence. An Amber Alert has already been issued. Sarah mentioned your name when she called, a neighbor confirmed Sarah showed up at your house, and financial records show a large sum of money was recently taken from your account."

Her jaw dropped open. "A large sum of money? I sent that to my in-laws to help with some medical bills."

"We'll have to confirm that."

"All of that was enough evidence to get a no-knock warrant?"

He stared hard at her. "Yes, it was, as a matter of fact. We couldn't risk you harming the girl."

This was getting old. How long were they going to keep her there? Were they going to lock her up? Would they question her until she confessed purely out of exhaustion to a crime she didn't commit?

Her head ached, her mouth was dry, and her muscles cried out for relief. She had to try a different approach here. She shifted, determined not to be defeated. "Please, you've got to listen to me. I'm innocent and the real bad guy is getting away with this."

"Who do you think the real bad guy is, Ms. Ryan?" Detective James leaned toward her again, obviously changing tactics himself.

His broad shoulders, she would guess, could either bulldoze someone or offer a landing place for tears. Muscles rippled beneath the material of his button-down shirt, confirming that he was not someone she wanted to mess with. His jaw was strong and tense with thought.

But right now, he leaned back, as if softening.

Her guard went up. This man wasn't her friend, and he would do whatever he had to in order to get answers. She'd be wise to remember that.

"I have no idea. But she didn't seem happy this morning. Maybe this was random. Maybe she ran away. Maybe she'll check in at any minute." Her voice escalated with each new sentence. "There's nothing else I can tell you."

Someone tapped on the one-way glass that

composed half a wall. The detective excused himself and stepped out of the room.

She sucked in some deep breaths. Detective James had perceptive eyes. He was watching her every move, just waiting for her to mess up. But she had no reason to walk on eggshells, she reminded herself. She'd done nothing wrong.

Would he ever believe her? She wasn't sure.

When he came back into the room a few minutes later, his face looked grimmer than before. The lines on his forehead had tightened. His eyes cooled. His shoulders were rigid. Something was in his hand.

He sat across from her and held up a device. Her phone, she realized. How had he gotten her phone? Had they gotten her computer, as well? She hoped not, although the classified projects she was working on should be safeguarded by the measures she'd put in place.

"Do you recognize this?" he asked.

She nodded stiffly. "Of course I do. It's mine."

His eyes flickered. "Do you recognize the message on the screen?"

She peered closer and sucked in a breath as she read the text message.

Meet me at 11:30. It's urgent.

Those were Laney's words. Written from her phone. Listed as coming from her. And the message was being sent to Sarah. She recognized her number.

Sarah replied:

I have school.

The person pretending to be Laney had written:

It's urgent.

Laney backed harder into her chair and shook her head. Someone was framing her—and they were doing a good job at it.

"I didn't send that," she muttered, knowing she was wasting her breath.

The detective's blue eyes were unyielding. "So you're saying someone took your phone and sent this for you?"

"I know it sounds far-fetched. But yes, that's exactly what I'm saying." But, in her gut, she knew this was far worse than she'd ever imagined.

Mark met his police captain in the hallway outside the interrogation room an hour later. Captain Hendricks was a stoic man who was twenty years Mark's senior, putting him at around fifty years old. The man had a light brown mustache and thick hair that matched. He was well respected in the department and was known as a man who could get the job done.

In the hours since her arrest and the interrogation, Laney hadn't caved in the least. If anything, she seemed even firmer in her insistence of her innocence. Honestly, he felt a little sorry for her. It was his job to get answers, but the woman seemed downright frightened.

"Let her go," Captain Hendricks said, staring through the glass at Laney.

Mark followed his gaze. She looked so innocent and unassuming. Like a computer geek—the cutest computer geek Mark had ever laid eyes on. But beneath all of that, who was hiding? Someone manipulative? Out for herself? Drowning in her own delusions?

"Let her go?" Mark asked, certain he hadn't heard correctly.

The captain put his hands on his hips and frowned—though the man always looked like he was frowning. "We don't have enough evidence to hold her."

Mark thought back to his sister. If the police had stayed on top of the case, she would still be alive right now. He never wanted that to be the case for one of his investigations. He'd vowed to be better than that.

"What about the phone call Mr. Novak got?" Mark reminded him. "The neighbor across the street who saw Sarah go into her house?"

The captain's gaze flickered to Mark, a touch of annoyance there. The captain didn't take kindly to being questioned. "It's all circumstantial. Keeping her here won't help us find the girl."

Mark drew in a deep breath, trying to pace his thoughts and remain respectful. "What are you thinking?"

The captain continued to stare at Laney, his eyes narrowing with thought. He was calculating something, Mark realized. But what?

"I want you to keep an eye on her, stick by her side," he finally said. "Hopefully she'll slip up and lead us right to Sarah."

"Did you check the records? Did Sol call her?" Many times in situations like these, the parents were the first suspect. Even though Sol's coworkers had verified he'd been at work all day, the detectives still needed to follow up.

"We confirmed he called her house phone."

"Her house phone? She said she was out walking. Why didn't he call her cell?"

"He claims he couldn't find the number. Anyway, we're going to focus on Laney in this case. There's more evidence against her."

Mark didn't like the way this was playing out. Though he was reserving his judgment on Laney's guilt, everything was pointing to her. Still, he had to follow the evidence. The team had just finished up at her house, but processing everything would take longer.

However, he'd been pressing her hard for answers. She hadn't once asked for a lawyer. She hadn't broken under the pressure.

That took a lot of strength.

Mark shifted, grateful he could speak openly to his captain. "What if she's not guilty, Captain?"

He raised a shaggy eyebrow. "Everything is pointing to the fact that she *is* guilty. The text message. The money. An eyewitness. If you weren't able to break her, I doubt she's going to at all."

Mark wasn't ready to let this drop. "Maybe she didn't break because she's innocent. She has no motive."

The captain's jaw flexed. "Her motive is there. Maybe it's buried down deep. But it's there. We're going to figure out what it is. Drive her home. See what you can get out of her. Play the good cop for once. See if she'll open up."

The problem was that Mark wasn't one for being fake. But he knew better than to argue with the captain. He nodded instead. "Yes, sir."

As he walked back toward the interrogation room, his shoulders felt heavier. Feeling even more brisk than before, he threw the door open and charged into the room. Laney jerked her head up from where it had been buried in her hands. Her eyes were red rimmed, as if she'd been crying. He inwardly flinched at the despair on her face.

"You're free to go," he announced.

Laney blinked. "What?"

"You heard me. You're free to go."

She stared at him a moment before quickly standing, almost as if she feared he'd change his mind. "Okay, then."

"I'll drive you home," Mark said.

"That won't be necessary. I can—"

"I insist," Mark said. "It's for your safety."

"My safety?" She blinked again. "You think I'm in danger?"

"People don't take kindly to child abductors. We need to take every precaution possible."

She stared at him another moment before nodding. "I see. That's fine, then."

Mark escorted her outside and into his car. Awkward tension crackled between them as he started down the road. Laney crossed her arms and stared out the window. She was obviously uncomfortable. So was he, for that matter. But he would do whatever it took to find the missing girl.

Rush hour traffic was in full swing, and the sun was already sinking low enough to cause a blinding winter glare as he headed west.

What if Laney was innocent? Allegations like these could turn her life upside down in a way that was hard to recover from.

Then he remembered the text message. He couldn't overlook that.

"Tell me again what you do for a living, Ms. Ryan."

She continued to stare out the window. "I work for a company called CybCorp."

"What exactly do you do for them?" They'd been over some of that already, but it seemed like a safer—friendlier—conversation than bringing up Sarah again.

Build trust. That was what he needed to do if he wanted to find answers. He'd had the opportunity to do that very thing with the man who'd killed his sister. If he could go back, he would go through whatever means necessary to make the man open up. Maybe Lauren would still be alive if he'd tried a little harder, if he'd pressed a little deeper, if he hadn't given people the benefit of the doubt. He hadn't been a cop back then, but he'd been in contact with the perp all along; he just hadn't realized it.

"I'm a programmer. CybCorp handles security for various businesses throughout the country. They're a smaller company, but they're reputable and they allow me to work from home."

"Must get lonely working at home."

She cut a sharp glance his way. "Let me guess—you're trying to trap me into confessing I abducted Sarah because I was lonely."

He shook his head. He actually hadn't been. He'd just tried to imagine what it would be like being single and also working alone. "I was just making conversation."

Her shoulders slumped slightly. "I like solitude, believe it or not."

"You said earlier that you're not married." He

already knew the answer, but he needed to develop some rapport with her. He'd read the police report—these details didn't appear relevant to the current investigation but were essential for putting together a psychological profile of Laney.

Laney frowned, staring out the window and rubbing her hands together. "No, I'm not. Not anymore. I'm widowed."

"I'm sorry."

"I'm sure you are." Her shoulders slumped even more, as if the burdens she carried overwhelmed her. "Sorry. You didn't deserve that one."

"What happened?" He kept his words soft and light.

"He survived Afghanistan, only to be killed by a home intruder here in the States. He'd only been home for three weeks when it happened." Her voice cracked and she finished with a deep gulp of air.

"I can't imagine. How long ago did that happen?"

A new somberness washed over her. "Three years. I was down in Norfolk at the time. I decided to get a fresh start here in Richmond afterward. There were too many memories down there. I had to get away."

"Makes sense. How did the two of you meet? A computer programmer and a navy SEAL."

"Proof that opposites attract, I suppose. I was actually in my last semester at MIT. I came with some friends down to Virginia Beach. I nearly got pulled out to sea by a riptide. Thankfully, Nate was there with some of his SEAL buddies. We were an unlikely pair, but Nate wasn't the type who always had to be macho and tough. He liked watching sitcoms and eating popcorn with melted mints at the bottom and playing old-school arcade games. We were inseparable after that. I graduated and got a job down in Norfolk so I could be near him. We got married four months later."

"Sounds like a nice story."

"Yeah, it is…it was." She absently rubbed her arms. "I know you probably won't believe me, but I was actually planning on being at that school banquet with Sarah tomorrow night. I'm incredibly sad that won't be happening. I'd been so looking forward to it."

"You like Sarah?"

"She's a great girl. Smart. Curious. Personable."

"Let me guess. She reminds you of yourself at that age."

A sad smile tugged at her lips. "Actually, she kind of does. It might sound crazy or maybe even expected. I don't know. But I guess I did see part of myself in her—my old self, at least. I'm not that person anymore."

He pulled to a stop in front of her house. It seemed the press hadn't caught wind of this case because they were surprisingly absent, and, at the moment, all the neighbors were inside their houses. Hopefully that meant no drama. The front door had been temporarily fixed—more to prevent an insurance claim than to be helpful.

Laney's hand went to the door handle, and she turned toward him. "Thank you."

He nodded toward her house. "I'm going to walk you in."

She visibly bristled at his announcement, as if the very idea offended her. "You don't have to do that."

"I do," he insisted. "I need to make sure your door was put back on its hinges and that no one is nosing around your place. Believe me, it happens. No more tragedies today."

She seemed to hesitate before nodding. "No more tragedies."

They climbed out of the car and started through the dry grass toward the porch.

At the door, Laney slid her key into the lock and paused, her lungs heaving with what he assumed was anxiety. Inside, there were probably too many bad memories for her. The invasion. The accusations. The interrogation that followed. Besides, the flash bang could shake up the steadiest of personalities.

"Let me go first," he said.

Before she could argue, Mark slipped past her. He kept his hand on his gun as he walked from room to room. This time, he saw the house through different eyes. No longer as a potential suspect's place, but instead as the residence of someone whose life had been turned upside down.

He saw pictures on the wall and on the entry-way table of Laney with a man whom he presumed to be her deceased husband. He saw the pictures of vacations together. Of Laney in front of the Christmas tree. Of the smiling couple standing in front of a backdrop of autumn-entrenched mountains.

She appeared to have had, at one time, a full life.

How did someone go from that to being such a loner? It seemed like a shame.

Of course, some people might say the same thing about him. He lived for his work. He had ever since his sister disappeared. He'd found it easier to pour all of his time and energy into a single cause than to let his thoughts linger on the tragedy in his life.

He had let one person in, though. Chrystal. He thought he might find healing in falling in love, but instead all he'd gotten was more heartache. She'd broken his trust just like his stepfather had. He was better off growing old alone than trusting someone else and being disappointed.

He walked back toward Laney, ready to give

her the all clear. Before he could, a gunshot pierced the front window.

He ran toward Laney and threw her on the ground, praying he wasn't too late to protect her.

THREE

Fear coursed through Laney as she heard glass shatter. As she realized a bullet was being fired. As she felt the detective throw her to the ground. As she quickly acknowledged the fact that someone was shooting at *her*.

Had the whole world gone crazy? How had a day that had started so ordinary turned into such a nightmare?

What she wouldn't do to turn back time. Not just on today. But to bring Nate back. To feel happy and safe again. To believe the whole world was in front of her.

But that wasn't possible.

Right now, she just had to survive. Take it day by day, moment by moment. That's how she'd gotten through the last three years.

Please, Lord, help me. Please.

"Are you okay?" Detective James yelled over her.

She could feel his heart pounding into her back. Or was that her heart? She couldn't tell.

Laney thought she said yes to his question, but she could hardly hear. Her ears rang. Life seemed to both blur and sharpen around her.

Another gunshot rang out. More glass shattered. The tension in her chest tightened as anxiety gripped her.

"Stay here," Detective James said.

She didn't have time to argue. He pushed away from her, his gun drawn, and approached the door.

Please don't let him get killed, she silently prayed, her palms pressed into the cool tile floor of her entryway. Shards of glass lay around her, a reminder of the gravity of the situation. Would they make it out of this alive?

The detective had been a thorn in her side, to say the least. He'd put her through the wringer at the station. Then again, she supposed he was just doing his job. But still, she didn't want to see him hurt. Especially not after he'd shown a halfway human side of himself in the car.

When she'd told him about Nate, his compassion had seemed sincere. But could she really trust the man? Or was he just trying to gain her faith in him because he hoped she'd open up about Sarah? If that was his goal, he was in for a rude awakening because she knew nothing.

"Sol, put the gun down," Detective James yelled.

Laney sucked in a quick breath. Sol? Sol was

shooting at her? Had the man lost his mind? Is that what grief and worry did to a person?

Laney knew the answer to that question: yes, it did. Grief could tear a person's heart in half and make them act erratically. Make them feel crazy, off balance, like they didn't care about anything while overly caring about everything.

"You released Laney. She took my daughter," Sol called from a far distance. "She'll get justice one way or another. I'll make sure of that."

"Shooting her would do no good. It won't help you find your Sarah," Detective James shouted, peering beyond the door frame. He was pressed against the wall, looking strong and capable with a gun in hand and wearing a black leather coat.

He could easily pass for one of those larger-than-life detectives on TV.

Laney shook her head. Where had those thoughts come from? And why now of all times?

"She needs to pay," Sol shouted.

"Let the law be the judge of that. If she's guilty, we'll find evidence to nail her. She'll be behind bars for life. Shooting her would be too easy."

Gee, thanks, she wanted to mutter. But if the detective's words saved her life, then so be it. Laney would clear her name herself if she had to. But she was never going to be able to do that under these circumstances. Here, she was a target. Her life was on the line. In fact, if the detective hadn't been there, that bullet could have taken her out.

She couldn't stay there tonight, she realized. It was too dangerous. But where would she go? She had no coworkers or family. Even church…though she attended each Sunday, she always slipped in late and left early. She was the poster woman for being reclusive lately.

Nate wouldn't have wanted this.

But it was too late to make any changes at the moment.

Detective James was on his radio, calling for backup, she realized. This situation could easily escalate and someone could end up hurt…or worse.

She felt frozen, though, unable to move from her spot on the floor. Too afraid to breathe even. She'd be dead right now if the detective wasn't with her.

But if Sol really thought she took Sarah, why would he try to kill her? Then he might not ever find his daughter. The man was acting irrationally. Come to think of it, he'd seemed distracted this morning, as well. Did he know more than he was letting on?

Her thoughts raced, as if playing in fast-forward. Who could have taken Sarah? Laney had no idea. In those quiet moments in the integration room, that's all she'd thought about. But she'd drawn no conclusions. She couldn't imagine any-one wanting to hurt the girl.

Please, let this be a misunderstanding.

What if Sarah had run away? Maybe she'd never been abducted at all. There could be a logical explanation for all of this. Would the police ever see that, though?

"Sol, we need you to put the gun down," Detective James called, still pressed against the wall. "Can you do that for me?"

"You're only going to let her go."

"We're going to keep investigating," he said. "We're not done yet."

Just then, red and blue lights flashed in the front yard. Backup had arrived, Laney realized.

A moment later, amidst the yelling outside, Detective James lowered his gun and approached her. His eyes were narrow with worry and concern. "Are you okay?"

She nodded and pushed herself from the ground, mindful of the shards of glass surrounding her. "Yes. Thank you. I…I don't think I'll stay here tonight."

"Probably a good idea."

She wiped her hands together, trying to ignore how badly they were trembling. None of this seemed real—yet it was. "I'm going to go grab some things. A change of clothes and my purse, at least."

"I can drive you to wherever you're going."

"You don't have to do that." She shook her head, another surge of panic rising in her. She desperately wanted someone to trust, but the detective wasn't that person. Besides, she needed to be there alone so she could grab her computer—if the police hadn't gotten it yet. Her work for the past nine months was there. In the wrong hands... She shuddered to think about what would happen if the program she'd developed ended up at the mercy of terrorists.

Detective James's gaze assessed her again, his calm demeanor somehow quieting her trembles. "Your hands are shaking badly. I don't think it's safe that you get behind the wheel."

"But...then I won't have a car." She desperately needed some type of control in her life. She felt like everything was being taken away, and so quickly at that.

"I'll have one of my guys bring it by later. Sound okay?"

Hesitantly, she nodded. If she protested too much, she'd probably only look guilty. Besides, she *was* awfully shaky. There was no need to add "auto accident" to an already horrible day.

"I guess so. Thank you."

Thirty minutes later, Mark pulled to a stop in front of a nice hotel in an upscale area outside of Richmond. He supposed that he shouldn't go out of his way for a potential suspect, but she was also potentially innocent. In fact, she was technically innocent until proven guilty. He intended to treat her as such.

He remembered Captain Hendricks's instructions to him: get on her good side and keep an eye on her. The captain hoped Laney would let something slip and she'd lead them to Sarah.

Mark was uncomfortable with deceit. If it could save a life then he was more inclined to justify his actions, though. He knew what it was like to be in Sol's shoes—to be sick with worry over a loved one's disappearance. He had to do whatever was necessary to get the girl back.

Their encounter with Sol still stained his thoughts. The man had been in Laney's front yard. The other officers had taken his gun and restrained him. But he'd still been able to hurl insults at Laney, calling her every name in the book. Her trembles had returned as he'd walked her to his car.

Laney glanced at the front door of the hotel and then back at Mark. "What's going to happen to Sol?"

"We're taking him down to the station."

Lines of worry appeared at the corners of her eyes. "I don't want to press charges. He's just reacting out of grief and anxiety. He doesn't need any more heartache on top of what he's already experiencing."

Her compassion impressed him, especially considering her situation at the moment. "I'll make sure to pass that along."

"Thank you for bringing me here. I appreciate it."

Before she could object again, he opened the door and stepped out. He was walking her inside, whether she liked it or not.

Almost hesitantly she seemed to step out. He sensed her shivering beside him as they ventured through the brisk winter air. Darkness had long since fallen, adding even more eeriness to an already tense situation. He grabbed her bag from the backseat and walked with her to the front desk.

"She needs a single," he told the clerk behind the counter. A table with coffee and cookies waited beside the check-in desk, and the scent of them both made his stomach rumble.

Lauren had loved chocolate chip cookies. She ate some every night before bed and never gained an ounce. At sixteen, she'd been as skinny as a rail without even trying.

The memory made his heart pang.

Laney pulled a credit card from her wallet and slid it across the counter. The police would be tracking all of her financial movements, of course. They were looking for anything that might give them a hint as to what was really going on here. Finances often showed a trail leading to answers.

With her room key in hand, Mark walked Laney

to the second floor of the building and watched as the door to her room clicked open. She turned toward him, trepidation in her gaze. "Thank you... I guess."

He understood her dilemma. She owed him thanks for saving her life, but after he'd interrogated and accused her, he could see why she wouldn't want to express her gratitude. Gratefulness and bitterness collided.

"Call me if you need anything," Mark instructed.

Her big, wide eyes looked up at him. "I don't have a phone."

"Use the hotel phone."

She nodded and looped a hair behind her ear. "Of course."

"Don't leave town."

"I can't. I don't have a car."

"We'll probably have more questions for you." He felt hesitant to leave—but why? Some kind of instinct urged him to protect her, yet he didn't want his compassion toward her to cloud his judgment. He had to keep it in check.

"I wouldn't expect any less."

Finally, he nodded. "Well, good night, then."

She seemed to force a smile. "Good night."

She closed the door, and Mark heard the locks click in place. With Laney safe and secure in her room, Mark started back down to his car. He'd scanned the hotel as they'd walked. There appeared to be three major exits. One at the front, one at the back, and one at the side near the pool area. It would be impossible to keep an eye on all three. But Laney's room was closest to the side exit, so he needed to position himself for the best angle of that door.

He suspected Laney wouldn't try anything, that she would stay put for the evening. She probably wouldn't be getting much rest—she looked too wound up and wired for that. But, just in case she did leave, he parked his car and started his surveillance. And in the meantime, he had his computer with him so he could do more research.

Out of curiosity, he typed in her name on a search engine. A news article about her husband's death popped up. He cringed at the details.

Nate Ryan had been found stabbed in his bedroom. The killer had never been caught, but authorities thought it was a home invasion gone wrong due to some missing jewelry and cash.

Laney had discovered her husband's body. He could only imagine how that had messed with her psychological well-being. Every detail of scenes like that would ingrain themselves into the minds of loved ones.

Mark still vividly remembered the first time he'd been called to the scene of a homicide. Every detail was burned into his mind. Since then, he'd learned to compartmentalize better. But he couldn't imagine finding a loved one like that.

It had been hard enough *hearing* about the murder of a family member. His sister, Lauren, had been abducted by their stepdad. Ralph had denied his involvement for weeks, but Mark had always known the truth. Six months later, Lauren's body was discovered in the woods by some hunters. She'd been shot. When his stepfather learned she'd been found, he'd quickly realized—maybe because of paranoia or guilt—that he would be a suspect. His solution was to kill himself—and Mark's mother.

According to his suicide letter, his stepdad had wanted his mom's attention all for his own. He and Lauren had been arguing and not seeing eye to eye. His stepdad had decided it would be easier to kill Lauren than it would be to try and work things out.

Anger had burned within Mark for months—for years, truth be told. He'd wished that things could be different, that he could have seen the signs earlier, that he could have predicted the future and saved both his mom and his sister.

Thankfully he'd found Jesus during that hard time. His relationship with God had turned his life around and had literally saved him from the depths of despair that threatened to consume him. He'd been in a bad place, but eventually all of that had led him to go into law enforcement. He'd abandoned a successful career in sales, searching for something that would be more fulfilling and make more of an impact. Being a detective had done just that.

He snapped from his thoughts as he saw movement in the distance near the side exit. Was that… Laney? He straightened, zeroing his gaze on the figure.

A woman stepped from the hotel, looked both ways, and then darted toward a gas station in the distance. It was definitely Laney, he realized. But what was she doing? If she was innocent, why was she acting so suspiciously right now?

He watched carefully as she hurried inside the gas station. She stayed there for six minutes until a cab pulled up and then she jumped into the backseat, and the car pulled away. Wasting no time, Mark followed the vehicle.

Was this the big moment? Would Laney lead him to Sarah? Or would that be too easy?

He stayed a safe clip behind them, trying not to tip Laney off that she was being followed. As the roads became familiar, he realized she was going back to her house. Had she remembered evidence she'd left there? Was she going back to destroy it?

He remained at the corner and watched as the cab dropped Laney off at the curb a moment later. She looked all around her before sprinting toward her house and slipping inside.

Mark waited until the cab pulled away before he approached the house. He withdrew his gun as he slunk toward the front door. He had no idea what he might find inside, and he had to use every precaution necessary. Maybe she really was dangerous, and his gut had been wrong.

He quietly twisted the door handle and pushed the door open. When he saw what was in Laney's hands, he drew his gun, realizing he'd been wrong about the woman all along.

FOUR

Laney gently placed a laptop computer onto the table in the foyer and drew her arms into the air as she spotted Mark there with his gun pointed at her. Even in the dark, she could see the accusation in his gaze. But there was something else there also. What was it?

Disappointment, she realized.

He'd followed her. Of course he had. Had she expected anything less?

"This isn't what it looks like," she muttered, quickly observing his gun. He was anticipating the worst and prepared to do whatever it took to find answers. She looked guilty—how could she convince him she wasn't?

"And what exactly am I looking at, Laney?" His eyes were ice-cold again as he stared at her with enough intensity to burn holes into her skin. "What are you doing here?"

Laney's heart lurched as she glanced at the computer. She'd been so close to leaving with the programs and data she had there. She couldn't let the wrong people get their hands on it. "There's nothing wrong with picking up a computer."

Doubt flickered in his gaze as he came closer, his gun still drawn. She hadn't turned the lights on in the house—another act that would make her look suspicious. But she'd been trying to remain on the down low.

However, that choice now left the house in darkness—eerie darkness. The shadows felt like they were moving and the silence in the in-between spaces of their conversation felt painful and long.

"The police had a warrant for your computers," Mark reminded her. "How'd they miss that one?"

Laney licked her lips, panic quelling inside her. This looked bad. Really bad. And she was a terrible liar.

"I know how this appears," she started. "But it's been here all along. If anyone had asked where I kept it, I would have told them."

"Unless you hid it and came back to destroy evidence on it."

Laney shook her head, desperate to get through to him. "There's no evidence on this. I use it for my work. It's my lifeline to the outside world."

He stepped closer and glared down on her. A whiff of evergreen tingled her nose and caused her heart to skip. The moment was short-lived as she quickly remembered the trouble she was in.

"Someone either really hates you and has gone through a lot of trouble to make you look guilty or you're guilty," the detective muttered. "I'm not sure which one yet. Based on the fact that you've been incredibly sneaky tonight, I'm learning toward the latter."

She swallowed hard, her throat dry.

"I'm going to need that computer."

Her fingers traced the top of her laptop. She'd rather the police have a hold of it than the bad guys. But still—there were things hidden on the hard drive that would raise suspicions. Thankfully, it would take the police department a while to locate that information. Maybe she could buy herself some time.

"Of course," she finally said. "It's like I said, I just remembered a few things I needed to pick up. That's the only reason I came here. I promise."

His gaze remained suspicious. "You could have called me."

"I figured you were home with your family." Her voice trembled with anxiety. "It really wasn't a big deal. At least, I didn't think it was."

As something dark crossed his face, she realized that any of his earlier goodwill was gone. She'd broken her trust with him and just diminished her chances of having someone in her corner.

"Why'd you go into that gas station?" he asked.

She didn't say anything. She knew how it would sound when she told him she had to buy a burner phone. She'd had no choice but to do so. She had to reach her CIA contact somehow. Nicholas was her only chance of getting help.

"I had to buy something," she finally said, sticking with the truth.

He shifted and narrowed his eyes. "What did you have to buy?"

She nibbled on her bottom lip a moment. There was no need to deny it. Certainly the police would end up checking her credit card records. They'd find out what she purchased one way or another.

"I bought a phone," she admitted. "You confiscated my cell, and I don't like to be without one. It's only smart as a single woman."

It was the truth—just not all of it.

Detective James shifted in front of her, his frame imposing and almost intimidating. "Who do you want to call? Your partner in crime maybe? The person who's helping you get away with this?"

"I just want to have the *ability* to call someone."

"Your hotel room has a phone."

Laney's shoulders slumped. Mark James didn't accept answers easily. She was certain that made him a good detective, but he frustrated her now. Her top-secret job was only working to make her look guilty, and she knew it.

"I wanted to call my boss, okay?" Laney crossed her arms over her chest, wishing something would go her way. Instead, life seemed to be working against her.

He finally lowered his hand from his gun. "Why?"

Her shoulders relaxed, but only slightly. "I might be missing work over the next few days. That's kind of important. I depend on my job to pay my bills. I can't afford to simply drop off the face of the earth without explanation."

"Again, you could have used your hotel phone." His calculating eyes continued to assess her.

Laney forced herself to raise her chin and not appear spooked by his interrogation. She had to be strong. Besides, she'd done nothing wrong. If she acted guilty, the detective would only have more ammunition against her. "I don't see where this is a big deal."

"It's a big deal because that phone you purchased will have an untraceable number. Maybe you want to make a ransom call with it. Or maybe you have an accomplice and you don't want us to know about your communications with him. I could continue to list more reasons, but I'm sure you can see my point."

Alarm rushed through her as the truth of his words settled in her mind. They were looking for anything possible to nail her. She had to be careful. "It's not like that. I promise."

Mark's gaze locked with hers. "I'm having a

hard time taking you at your word, Laney. You've been less than honest with me."

At the moment, she felt both dwarfed by his presence and like she wanted to shrink and hide. "I haven't lied. I just didn't realize I needed to run these things past you."

The detective narrowed his eyes. "You're our number-one suspect. We're watching your every move. Surely you realize that. I need you to turn over that phone to me."

She raised her chin. She had no one to fight for her. That meant she had to fight for herself. It was that or let herself go down for a crime she didn't commit. Still, she had to choose her battles.

Begrudgingly, she slapped the phone into his hands. "Fine. But you're wasting your time investigating the wrong person. Meanwhile, the real culprit is probably burying himself deeper, which lessens your opportunity to find him."

They stared off for a moment, neither saying anything.

She waited, wondering if the detective would arrest her again.

Mark's phone buzzed. He kept his eyes on Laney as he pulled it from his belt. The woman wasn't telling him everything, and he wasn't ready to let this drop. But the phone call was from his partner, and he hoped Jim might have something new to move this case along.

"We have new information," Jim said.

"What's that?" Mark didn't dare pull his gaze off the woman in front of him.

"Ms. Ryan's in-laws never got that money she said she sent to them. Said they didn't know anything about it."

Mark watched as Laney stood against the wall, looking as rigid as a statue. Had his gut instinct been wrong? Was she guilty and trying to play him for a fool?

"Interesting. Any record of where it went?"

"Into a secret account," Jim said. "The amount was just deposited yesterday. It would be the perfect amount of money to get away from everything. Ten thousand dollars would last a long time."

His stomach twisted with disgust. Laney was obviously a great liar. The best criminals had looks that were deceiving. They hid in plain sight under the guise of being a good citizen. They won awards. They had no police record. Their pasts seemed to provide alibis within themselves.

Wolves in sheep's clothing, he reminded himself.

They were out there, just waiting to strike.

He rubbed his jaw, more annoyed than ever. "How does the captain want us to handle this?"

"Same protocol. Keep an eye on her. He's hoping she'll lead us right to Sarah. If she really cares about the girl like she claims, she'll have to get back to her eventually to check on her and give her food."

"Not if she has a partner," Mark said.

"I thought of that. But the woman's a loner. Who would she be working with?"

"I'm not sure."

"We're looking into her records and trying to get in touch with her boss," Jim said. "The number she gave us keeps on coming up as disconnected."

"I'll keep all of that in mind," Mark muttered. That was another strike against her. They continued to add up. "Thanks."

Mark hung up and turned to Laney. Her eyes were wide with anticipation, as if she knew something was wrong. He wasn't letting her off the hook this time.

"You want to rethink your story?"

She stared a moment before shaking her head. She rolled back her shoulders, as if finding some kind of internal courage. "No, I don't. I told you the truth."

"Then explain why your in-laws know nothing about that money you supposedly sent to them."

Her eyes became even wider. "I did send it to them. Just two days ago. Ten thousand dollars. My father-in-law has been out of work and dealing with multiple health issues. It seemed the least I could do. Nate would have wanted me to do it. I used part of his life insurance policy that I'd been saving for a rainy day."

"The money never got to them."

Her forehead wrinkled with confusion. "I was going to surprise them. I had a cashier's check cut and sent out. I have no idea why they haven't received it."

"Can you explain why another bank account was opened in your name and the money was deposited there?"

Her lips parted. "You can't be telling the truth. I didn't do that. It doesn't make any sense."

"Computer records say you did."

"Computer records are wrong." She crossed her arms. "They can be manipulated."

"How do you know that?"

"I have my PhD in computer science. I'm a software engineer, in simple terms. That's why."

Mark shifted, determined not to let this go. "Why isn't your boss answering his phone?"

She tilted her head. "He hasn't answered for me, either. Maybe something came up. It's the only thing I can think of."

"Maybe that's because the company doesn't exist."

Her eyes widened with something close to panic. "Of course it exists. I've worked there for three years. Can't you see that I'm being set up? I know you probably don't believe me, but I'm telling you the truth."

"Who would have had access to your information to do something like this?"

She shook her head. "I feel like a broken record, but I truly have no idea. Someone who's better at computers than I am…" Her voice trailed and her eyes got a faraway look.

"What are you thinking?"

She fidgeted. "I work with computers and programming. If I could access my computer—"

"Then you could potentially delete more evidence against you."

"I didn't."

"Maybe you're working with someone?"

She shook her head more adamantly now. "No! I'm not. At least give me the chance to prove myself."

"As soon as my partner is able to go before a judge, we'll have a warrant for your arrest."

Panic quelled in her gaze, and she gripped the wall again, as if she needed it to hold her steady. "No! Please. I just need time. I want to find Sarah just as much as you. Maybe even more."

"There's something you're not telling me, Laney, and I intend to figure out what that is."

She raised her chin. "If I'm not under arrest, then I need to ask you to leave."

He stared back. "I'm not letting you out of my sight."

"You're violating my rights. Unless you're arresting me, then leave."

He considered his words carefully. His hands were tied there. The woman was right: he couldn't force her to let him stay. But his boss had ordered him to keep an eye on her. "You're making a mistake if you send me away."

She stared back, a fire igniting in her gaze. "No, you're the one making a mistake here. And I'm going to prove it."

Just as he stepped out of her house, an explosion rattled windows.

FIVE

Laney rushed out her door and gasped when she saw the flames burning from the center of her yard. "What…?"

A vehicle squealed away. Mark quickly called for backup before grabbing Laney's arm. "Stay back."

"But what…?"

"Molotov cocktail," he explained. "It's a type of homemade bomb. Maybe someone wants to let you know you're not welcome in the neighborhood anymore. It's not all that unusual in situations like these."

She narrowed her eyes at Mark. No one would think she was guilty if the police hadn't taken her in. They were wasting so much time on her when the real kidnapper was getting away.

Mark paused for long enough to respond to someone on his phone. The flames had quickly died down—the explosion more for a surprise effect than to cause damage. Well, it had worked. Laney was more shaken than ever.

She had to be proactive here. Sarah's life was on the line, but so was Laney's. She'd learned a long time ago she couldn't wait around for other people to save the day. If she was going to prove her innocence and help Sarah, she had to make the most of her time.

Laney stormed toward the back of the house.

"What are you doing?" Mark called, following after her.

"I'm looking for evidence that your guys aren't searching for."

"If you're innocent, then you won't mind if I tag along."

She turned toward him, her eyes blazing. "Be my guest."

She was all too aware that he was on her heels as she went into her backyard. She desperately longed to get on her computer, to do what she did best: researching. Maybe she could contact Nicholas through her email. Maybe the agency would hire a lawyer for her or give her advice on how to manage this situation.

That computer was like an appendage. It was her work, her livelihood, her fun, her connection with the outside world. While other girls had been doing their hair and makeup, she'd been writing code. The odd quirk hadn't gained her many friends, but eventually she'd gotten a full-ride scholarship to MIT. She'd been sought after by the biggest and best companies.

None of her professors would have predicted this.

"What exactly are you looking for?" Mark asked.

"I have no idea. But somewhere here, there's evidence that tells a different story than the one you guys have put together. I intended to find out what it is."

"Go for it."

She turned her flashlight app on her phone and shone the beam along the ground. No doubt the police had trampled any evidence in their effort to nab her. But maybe there was something they'd missed.

Common sense sometimes eluded her, but she was book smart and had attention to details. Her brain, it seemed, sometimes worked like a computer. She was always processing facts but not always great at interpreting them.

Where else could she look?

If Sarah really had come into Laney's house while she was gone, then where had she disappeared to? No one had seen her leave out the front door. But Laney's backyard had a privacy fence that stretched along the property. Anything happening back there would be concealed. However, neighbors surrounded her on all sides.

She headed outside and began walking along

the property line, looking for anything that might offer a clue. It all seemed useless, but she couldn't give up. She had to do something!

If people had been back there, then they would have to leave through the fence. Otherwise, the only gate led to her driveway and anyone could have seen.

She paused by one area of the fence. Something there caught her eye. The section of pickets was slightly uneven with the rest. They hadn't been like that before. She was certain of it.

She leaned closer. Along the edges there were pry marks.

Pry marks.

What if…?

"What are you thinking?"

Mark's voice pulled her away from her thoughts. She'd nearly forgotten he was there he'd been so quiet and observant. Was he waiting for her to mess up? To slip up and reveal something that she hadn't admitted yet?

She stared at the fence, her mind working like a computer processing new commands. Slowly, the information formed a picture. "What if someone lured Sarah to my house? Maybe once she got inside, they knocked her out or restrained her somehow. Then they took her out the backyard and through this section of fence."

"How did someone have access to your house? Who else has a key?"

She refused to frown. "No one. But it's not that hard to jimmy locks."

"You don't have an alarm? That's usually the first thing people do when they've had a home invasion."

This time the frown tried hard to break through, but she continued to fight it. The detective was sharp; she'd give him that. "I do. But I've only been using it at night."

"Why would someone go through all of that trouble?"

"That's the question *you're* supposed to be figuring out." She didn't bother to look at his reaction. Instead, she pointed in the distance. "Sol's property backs up to a section of woods. Maybe the kidnappers had a car waiting back there."

"That's a lot of work when someone could have grabbed her at the bus stop."

Not if someone's trying to frame me.

She kept that thought silent—for now—and locked gazes with Mark. "So what do you think?"

Mark stared into space a moment. He pressed his lips together in thought as if battling with himself. Finally, he nodded. "I've got to say that I can't discount that possibility. I'll have some of my men check it out."

"Thank you."

"Don't thank me yet," he warned. "And you might want to seriously think about hiring a lawyer."

Just then, car doors closed out front and more flashing lights appeared.

"Come on," Mark said, cupping her elbow and leading her toward the back door.

"Where are we going?"

"I need you to wait inside while I talk to the guys out front. Stay there until I get back. Understand?"

She nodded. "Understood."

Maybe—just maybe—the detective would eventually believe her. Maybe the police would start looking in the right direction, focusing their efforts on the real kidnapper instead of Laney.

She prayed to God that she wasn't asking too much.

Please, Lord, give them wisdom. And watch over Sarah.

Mark's comrades in arms had managed to catch the man who'd tossed the Molotov cocktail into Laney's front yard. Mark had memorized his license plate, and the police had quickly tracked him down at his house two blocks over. As he suspected, the man—a neighbor—had wanted to show his displeasure that a "kidnapper" had been released into his neighborhood. The community often wanted to show their own justice at the atrocities that affected them, especially when they felt like the police weren't doing their jobs.

The man had no prior history, but he'd acted as a vigilante on behalf of the neighborhood. He had a background first in the military and currently as a security guard, which he felt gave him a license to take justice into his own hands.

At the moment, fire trucks lingered outside Laney's home, officials making sure there was no further danger from the bomb that was thrown, two police cars still remained, and an ambulance had even come, just in case. Neighbors peeked out their windows, curious about the circus going on outside their homes.

When he walked back inside, he stopped in the foyer. Laney held a metal object in her hand and swept it across pictures on the dining room wall. The machine started to beep by a mirror and she set what he now recognized as a metal detector on the table before shoving the mirror aside.

"What are you doing?" Mark's hands went to his hips. Had this woman lost her mind? Was she paranoid?

She plucked something from the wall and stepped back, a deep frown on her face as she stared at the bug-sized object.

"I'm looking for these." She raised the small, metallic device in her hands up to the light so Mark could get a better look.

"What is that?" Mark had an inkling, but that just didn't fit with the situation or with Laney, for that matter. He still remained cautious, hoping the woman wasn't crazy.

Fire lit her eyes as she met his gaze. "This is a camera. Someone's been watching me. They've been learning my routine. Listening to my conversations. Who knows what else."

She dropped it on the ground and smashed it with her foot with more vengeance than was probably necessary.

He started to stop her, reached for her, but finally dropped his hand and scowled. "If what you said is true, you just ruined our chances of tracking down whoever left it here," he muttered.

She frowned and stared at the hardware on the ground. "You're right. I was hasty. I just couldn't stomach someone being able to record any more of my life or this conversation, for that matter. I'm sorry."

"How did you know?" He tried to put the pieces together, what he knew about Laney, what he knew about this kidnapping. Something wasn't fitting, and that realization caused unease to stir in him. What exactly was going on here?

Laney held up the metal detector. "This is a long story."

"I have time." He crossed his arms. She wasn't getting out of answering that easily.

"It was just a gut feeling. I can't explain it."

"Normal people don't have 'gut feelings' that

they're being bugged." Paranoid people—maybe. But paranoid people were hardly ever correct. Laney, somehow, was.

She squirmed. "I've always been overly cautious. My husband was a SEAL."

"Keep going," he insisted.

"There were threats against the families of SEALs. We did some defense classes. Any other information, you'll have to talk to his commander."

"And the cameras? I suppose they trained you on how to find those also?"

The same fire flashed in her gaze again. "You're avoiding the real issue here. Someone has been surveilling me and now I'm being set up. That was the third camera I found."

He crossed his arms, trying to remain cautious. His unease was quickly turning into alarm. Why would someone have planted these in her house? Or was this just a scheme by Laney to take the attention off herself?

He rubbed his chin, wishing that metal detector was a lie detector instead. "If what you're saying is true, they went through a lot of trouble to make you look guilty."

"You don't have to tell me that. I think I've been a target all along. Who knows how long these have been here."

"You really think someone has been spying on

you?" If she was right about all of this, the police department should hire her. Right now.

An odd look came across her face and she stepped back. "How else would you explain it?"

"I don't know," he finally said.

Another unreadable emotion seized her expression and she nodded stiffly. "I see. Well, if this doesn't prove to you that I'm being set up, then I don't know what else will."

"How do I know you didn't plant those things while I was outside talking to the other officers?"

Just then, someone else stepped into the house. Relief seemed to wash over Laney at the interruption. They both turned and looked at the officer, who shifted uncomfortably.

"We found footprints, sir," the officer said.

Mark hurried toward him. "What do you mean?"

"Footprints go through the woods, probably to a car that was waiting on the other side of the property. I think your theory was correct. That's how someone got away with the girl."

Mark rubbed his chin. Laney had been right. Was that because she was guilty? Was she setting herself up to be both the victim and the hero, all while carefully manipulating the situation?

His ex had been the queen of manipulating people and situations. He vowed he'd never find himself entangled with that kind of person again. He'd be wise to be on guard now.

"How was this missed earlier?" Mark asked.

The officer's face reddened. "We're not sure. Mr. Novak's yard was checked but not this one. There was a lot going on."

"I want casts of those prints."

"Yes, sir. We're bringing out a crew to set up lights so we can take pictures, as well."

He reached toward the table and grabbed the computer. Laney frowned and crossed her arms, which only confirmed that the device needed to be checked out.

"I need you to log this as evidence," he told the officer, giving Laney a pointed look.

She raised her chin in defiance.

As the officer left, Mark turned toward Laney. "I'll have a crew come in and search your house for other bugs. For now, let me take you back to the hotel. There's nothing else we can do here."

She let out a long breath. "Fine."

Against his better instincts, he paused a moment. "You want to grab a bite to eat first? I don't think you've had anything since we took you in earlier today, have you?"

She hesitated a moment before saying, "Sure."

"Let's go, then. Maybe we'll both feel better."

"I didn't do this, Detective James." Her voice sounded pleading and earnest, just as it had every time.

He wanted to assure her that he believed her.

But he couldn't do that. Instead, he mumbled, "I hear what you're saying."

Only time would provide either of them with answers.

Laney didn't know what kind of game Mark was playing, but she was confident he was up to something. He didn't trust her, he wondered if she was guilty, yet he was being kind. Maybe he was trying to play on her sympathies. Laney only knew she had to remain on guard.

He'd taken her to a diner down the road. There was hardly anyone there at that time of the day— it was already past midnight. The place smelled like fast food, and something about the plentiful carafes beckoned patrons to drink coffee out of the establishment's chipped porcelain mugs.

Laney had ordered an omelet with home fries. She dipped a potato into a glob of ketchup and took a bite. No food tasted good. She wasn't sure when that would change.

Her mind kept turning over facts and scenarios and motives. Nothing made sense. Her thoughts all moved too rapidly, too frantically almost.

Why wasn't Nicholas calling her back? He'd be able to explain so many things. He'd be able to take some of the suspicion off her. Then maybe she could honestly explain to Mark why she'd had that metal detector. Why she'd thought to sweep her house for bugs. Why someone might be setting her up.

As someone who worked for the CIA, this was a part of her basic training. It was a part of spy games. She was a target. Her work was a target. She'd learned from her superiors how to look for bugs and cameras.

She expected to get demands any time now from the person framing her. *Sell us your information or we'll kill Sarah. Tell us what you've been up to or we have more evidence against you. Share US secrets or we'll make sure your life ends.*

"What are you thinking about?" Mark's voice pulled her out of her thought vortex. He'd ordered a slice of apple pie and coffee, but he mostly picked at the food, almost as if he'd ordered it just to be social.

For some strange reason, she longed to pour everything out to him. To pour everything out to someone she could trust. At the moment, she felt so alone.

If only Nate was there. He'd know what to do. He'd know just what to tell her to make her feel better, to make her believe that everything would be okay. But nothing had been right since he'd died. And nothing ever would.

"I'm thinking about how when I woke up this morning, I had no idea how my day would turn out."

He pressed his lips together, like he knew better than to smile but wouldn't allow himself to frown. "Life can change in an instant. You want to tell me about that metal detector yet? Or do you really want me to track down your husband's former commander?"

She drew in a deep breath, trying to compose herself. She had cover stories in place, but she hated lying. Hated it. "I'll tell you as much as I can. But it basically boils down to this—there were lots of threats against my husband's SEAL team, especially after one of his raids."

"One of his raids?"

She nodded. "He wouldn't tell me all the details. Everything was hush-hush. But his commander called me at one point, and said that several people who were a part of this terrorist organization Nate had helped to take down had vowed revenge against the SEAL team. Nothing seemed to have come of it. But in the weeks following, I kept feeling like someone was watching me. Another wife of one of the SEAL members actually found a bug in her home. That's when I got the metal detector. I didn't want anyone overhearing my phone calls with my husband, especially if we were discussing sensitive information."

"His line had to be secure."

She nodded. "But mine wasn't."

"I didn't think they were allowed to discuss sensitive information—not even with their wives."

She frowned. "They're not. But we had to take every precaution to protect the SEAL team, as well as family. It was extreme but necessary."

"You didn't live at this house with your husband, did you?"

"I didn't. But old habits die hard. SEAL families can be targets, even when they're widowed and childless."

He shifted, taking another sip of coffee. "So you think this is one of your husband's enemies who's setting you up for this?"

She set her fork down, giving up on her omelet. "I'm not saying anything. I have no idea what's going on. I just know that there are people that hate me because of my husband. It doesn't matter that he's dead. I've always been cautious. I'm even more cautious now that I'm a single woman whose husband died in a home invasion."

His eyes softened and he wrapped his fingers around his porcelain mug. "I'm sorry."

She nodded, trying to hold herself together. The thought was still hard to swallow sometimes. How could anyone have killed her strong and brave husband? He'd fought with everything in him to stay alive, but he hadn't been armed and the home invader had been.

The police had ruled that his murder wasn't connected with Nate's military service, but Laney had always wondered. The whole thing had always seemed so strange—that people would kill in order to steal some jewelry that was probably worth less than a thousand dollars.

She pushed her food away. "You know, I think I'm ready to get back to the hotel. I'm awfully tired."

"Sounds good." He dropped some bills on the table and stood. "Let's go."

The hotel was only less than a mile away, and the ride there was silent. When they arrived, Mark insisted on walking her inside. She'd expected it.

Each step felt heavy as she dragged herself up toward her room. She needed time alone to process all of this—though she knew this was going to take a lot of time to swallow and digest.

At her door, she turned and offered the detective a curt nod. "Thank you."

"I'll be waiting outside in the morning. I'll give you a ride."

"I'd expect no less." She offered a tight smile.

"Good night, Laney."

"Good night, Detective." She slipped her key card into the handle and heard a click. She stepped inside the dark room, careful to engage each lock behind her, before leaning against the door for a moment, trying to control her heartbeat.

Maybe some water would help. She took a step forward, resigned to her mundane plan.

Before she reached the bathroom, someone lunged from the shadows and tackled her.

SIX

Laney's heart jumped into her throat, her pulse racing out of control as the intruder slapped a hand over her mouth. In one easy motion, he pinned Laney on the floor until she could hardly move.

Despite his efforts, she threw her shoulders back and forth. Kicked. Tried desperately to pull her hands out of his grasp.

Even if she couldn't get away, maybe Mark would hear her outside and realize something was wrong.

But it was no use. The intruder had been careful. He'd been quiet and methodical and moved like a well-trained soldier.

Even as she fought back, hardly a sound escaped. There was nothing around to grab or to kick. Nothing but empty space.

Focus, Laney. Focus.

The man wore a black mask, and her room was dark. She couldn't make out anything about him. He said nothing, just stared at her with lifeless black eyes, waiting patiently for her to stop thrashing about.

Panic surged and then surged again. What was he going to do to her? Why was he here? Who was he?

The questions raced through her, each one more urgent than the last.

Finally, she stopped struggling, realizing she needed to reserve her energy for whatever would happen next. Maybe he'd talk to her and voice his threat or ultimatum. There was no way she could overpower him, so maybe she could reason with him.

She was just trying to convince herself of things that would never happen, she realized. She was offering herself platitudes in an effort to survive.

Please, Lord. Please. I need You now, more than ever. Help me!

"Good girl," the man whispered. "Cooperation will make this easier."

She flinched, his tone making her blood go cold. Something snapped inside her at his implication that she was already defeated.

No! She couldn't cooperate. Never!

Her resolution gave her a second wind. She threw her shoulders back and attempted to kick her legs. She'd fight to the end. She had no other choice.

"Calm down," he whispered. "We wouldn't want anyone to hear."

She wished she could speak. To plead for her life. To call for help. But his hand remained pressed against her mouth so tightly that her teeth ached.

Finally, he spoke again. "These accusations against you have taken a toll, haven't they? It's all starting to get to you."

She remained frozen and still. What was he getting at? Was this another community member who wanted to take justice into his own hands? Was this an enemy of her husband's coming after her? Could this be the man who'd taken Sarah?

Nothing made sense.

"Everyone will understand how the pressure got to you," he continued. "It would get to anyone."

Laney's heart ratcheted even more. Something bad was about to happen. She was sure of it.

Her body tightened in anticipation. How would she get out of this? If only she had a gun. If she had something to defend herself. But she didn't. She felt helpless.

The man reached into his pocket and fiddled with something before bringing his hand up near her face. "Open wide."

Before she could grasp what he was doing, he shoved something in her mouth.

Pills, she realized.

His other hand came down on top of her lips. She faught against him, struggled to stop herself from consuming whatever he'd forced into her mouth.

"Be a good girl. Swallow."

She rocked her head back and forth, determined not to give in. What kind of pills had they been? They were already starting to dissolve in her mouth, leaving a bitter taste on her tongue.

These pills would kill her, she realized. It would look like a suicide. Like she'd given into internal pressure. That was the man's plan.

She couldn't let that happen.

He pressed harder on her mouth. Shook her. Tilted her head.

"We can do this the easy or the hard way," he whispered.

She shook her head again, determined to let him know that she'd never cooperate. Never.

Just then, he motioned across the room. Another man appeared from the shadows.

Sweat broke out across her forehead. This had all been planned. All of it.

The man brought a bottle of water. Before she could stop him, the first man moved his hand, grabbed the bottle and began pouring the liquid into her mouth. She swallowed, unable to fight the urge any longer.

She coughed and sputtered, nearly drowning from the water. Unable to breathe. Certain she was going to choke.

No!

"Good girl," the first man soothed, satisfaction in his voice.

He placed his hand over her mouth again, keeping her quiet. Keeping her immobile. Waiting for the effects to begin.

"Now I just have to wait for this to kick in. It will only take a few minutes. Then all your troubles will be over."

No. It couldn't end like this. But how could she right the situation? She couldn't—not with the man standing over her.

A cry rose in her chest. In a few minutes, she could meet her maker. She didn't feel ready for that. Not yet. She still had more work to do there.

Behind her, a knock sounded at the door. "Laney? It's me. Mark. Sorry to bother you, but I have a question that can't wait."

She froze. Mark. Mark could help her.

Please, give him the foresight to know I'm in trouble.

The man on top of her froze also. He glanced at his friend, some kind of silent communication happening between them.

Quickly, Mark. Think quickly.

She was already feeling drowsy. Otherworldly. Like she wasn't herself.

The medication was now taking effect. Soon, she'd lose consciousness. With this man hovering over her, she couldn't even force herself to vomit and purge the drug from her system. She was at his mercy.

Mark knocked again.

She held her breath, waiting for the men to react. Would they flee? That would give her the chance to try and save herself at least.

Her eyes felt droopy. Heavy.

No!

"Laney, are you there? Could you open up, just for a minute?"

Just as a last speck of hope ignited in her, her body went limp and she lost consciousness. It was too late.

Worry ricocheted through Mark. Why wasn't Laney answering? Sure, they weren't friends. She had no obligation to him. She could even be in the shower.

But none of those things felt right. Something was wrong. He felt certain of it. It was too quiet on the other side of that door. He'd only left her five minutes ago.

As he reached the lobby doors he'd gotten a phone call about her computer. Their tech guy said it looked too clean, like she'd erased any personal information. He wanted to ask Laney about that himself. He had to admit that the idea of seeing her again intrigued him.

At least, it had initially. Now all he felt was concern.

Making a quick judgment call, he rammed his shoulder into the door. It didn't budge. He backed up farther, built up as much momentum as he could, and rammed into the door again. This time the door frame cracked. One more time should do it. He repeated his previous actions and the door opened.

He hurried inside. Laney was lying on the floor. Pills were scattered around her head, her hand. A bottle of water spilled onto the floor beside her.

She'd tried to kill herself.

He knelt beside her and slapped her cheeks. "Laney, can you hear me? Laney?"

She was unresponsive.

Dear Lord, help her. Please!

Quickly, he called for backup. She needed medical attention. Now. Three minutes ago.

With support on the way, he dropped his phone and carried Laney into the bathroom. He turned on the cold water and placed her under the spray of the shower.

"Wake up, Laney. Wake up."

She moaned, and hope surged in him. Maybe there was a chance.

How could she have done this? They'd just talked. She'd seemed sad, but not desperate. He'd never guessed that this might happen. Maybe he should have stayed with her longer, tried to monitor her more closely.

Did this indicate her guilt? Could she not take the pressure anymore?

"Laney, can you hear me?" he asked as cold water pounded her face, as it dampened the sleeves of his button-down shirt.

She shifted back and forth as if fighting with herself before moaning again.

"Laney, this isn't the answer. Don't stop fighting," he urged her.

"Men…" she muttered.

He stiffened. "Men what?"

"Hotel…" She opened her eyes for long enough to glance at the door.

"What are you talking about?"

Her eyes closed again.

Before she could say anything else, the doors burst open. The paramedics were there. They shoved him out of the way and began working on her. As they did, Mark stepped back and let them do their job, knowing they were far more capable than he was.

In the blink of an eye, they wheeled her out the door. He wanted to go with her, but he knew his time was better served here investigating. He prayed she would be okay.

"Jamie, keep an eye on her," Mark ordered one of the officers. "Don't let her out of your sight. Do you understand? No matter what happens."

"Yes, sir."

As they walked away, Mark paced the room.

Men. Hotel.

What was Laney talking about? Had someone done this to her? But how? He'd burst into the room and hadn't seen anyone.

His gaze traveled across the space. There was another door there, one that connected to an adjoining room. He walked over and twisted the lock. It didn't budge.

Had someone escaped that way?

He squatted down to better examine the floor. There was an impression of a footprint there. On the deep blue carpet. A large footprint. A man's.

Paramedics? No. They hadn't come that far into the room. He felt certain.

It was near the second door.

His heart rate surged.

Had someone else been in there? He needed to find out. Because if someone had just tried to kill Laney, then this whole case would be turned upside down.

He rushed downstairs and, several minutes later, he was set up in a back room with full access to video footage from the hotel.

He stared at the computer screen, fast-forwarding and rewinding several recordings. The images didn't cover every single space in the hallway—there were blind spots—but the angles did show most of the floor where Laney's room had been.

He leaned forward in the plush leather chair of the hotel manager's office. The TV in front of him recorded images from the many, many cameras situated throughout the establishment.

The manager had helped him to find the right locations and time, and then he'd left Mark to review the images on his own.

He played and replayed the same footage over and over, looking for answers. Determined not to miss anything. Studying each clip detail by detail.

He watched himself drop Laney off at her room. Walk away. And then there was nothing. No one.

If only he'd known then what he knew now. If only he'd been able to anticipate that someone else was in the room. If only he'd insisted on checking things out, of thinking of Laney as a victim instead of a suspect.

Something tugged at his subconscious and he straightened.

He stared down at the time stamp at the bottom of the footage.

Wait a minute.

He rewound the video again.

Part of it had been erased! The time jumped from 12:12 to 12:24.

What exactly is going on here?

He watched it several times, just to be certain. This tape had definitely been altered. He didn't know how. He didn't know by whom. But there was more at play here than met the eye.

"Excuse me," he called to the hotel manager.

"Could you tell me who's checked into the room next to 301?"

"Yes, sir." The man hurried back into the room and typed away on his computer before mumbling something underneath his breath. "It says here his name is John Smith."

"John Smith? I need the rest of his information. Starting with when he checked in."

"He checked in about an hour after Ms. Ryan did."

Wasn't that interesting? A coincidence? Mark didn't think so. Someone was targeting Laney.

"I need these videos for our specialists to analyze—and for evidence. I also need you to pull up any footage on him from the time he checked in."

"No problem."

"Has anyone else had access to the security room or tapes this evening?"

He shook his head. "No, no one but me and I've been working the front desk all night."

Mark stood, feeling more determined than ever. "I need to go check out the room now."

"Here's a key card."

Without wasting any more time, Mark hurried upstairs. The crime scene unit was still pulling evidence from Laney's room. He grabbed two officers to help him before bursting into the room next door.

It was empty. And it was like no one had ever been there.

Except for more footprints.

He knelt on the floor next to the adjoining door. Footprints that matched the one from Laney's room.

He needed to get the CSIs in there, as well.

And then he had to get to the hospital and check on Laney. He prayed with everything inside him that she was okay.

SEVEN

Laney heard someone calling her name and opened her eyes from a sluggish, drug-enhanced daze. How long had she been out? An hour? Two? She had no idea.

Her mind felt foggy and her thoughts uncertain. Where was she? How had she gotten there?

She flinched as memories began hitting her.

The hotel room. The men who were there. The drugs.

She'd almost died.

Tears pressed at the corners of her eyes as panic tried to seize her. No, she was okay now. She was in the hospital.

A new set of memories and emotions hit, each one still fuzzy, almost like a dream instead of reality.

Medical procedures. Pain. Desperation.

Then peace. Healing. Restoration.

If Mark hadn't come back to the hotel room when he had, she *would* be dead right now. The cleaning crew would have found her in the morning and assumed she'd taken her own life. And the deadly plan against her would have been carried to completion.

Someone said her name again, and she pulled her eyes open, coming back to reality. Slowly, Mark's face came into view. His once barely there beard now filled out his cheeks and chin. His hair—which was short and no-frills—still looked fresh.

Seeing him caused heat to rise on her cheeks.

She was attracted to him, she realized. She had to nip that in the bud. Now.

The concerned look in his eyes didn't make her decision any easier, though.

"How are you, Laney?"

"Someone…tried to…kill me," she whispered, her throat sore. Now he had to believe her that she was being set up.

"I know."

She blinked. Had she heard him correctly? "You do?"

He nodded. "He got in and out through the room connected to yours." He leaned closer. "Laney, do you remember anything about the man who did this to you?"

She coughed, wishing she felt like herself. Wishing her brain still didn't feel fuzzy. Wishing none of this had transpired.

"Do you need some water?" Mark grabbed the

glass beside her bed and held the straw to her lips. She tried to take it from him, but it was no use. Her arms weren't cooperating. When would this medication wear off?

"I've got it," he said.

For a moment, she felt self-conscious. It was such a simple act, yet somehow it felt intimate, like something that should be reserved for loved ones. Despite that, her throat was desperate for moisture, so she took a sip.

As the liquid refreshed her, she had a spurt of renewed energy. "The man…he was waiting in the shadows. He tackled me. Forced the pills into my mouth."

"You said *men* when I found you. Why?"

"There were two of them. One was almost trying to remain hidden. But when I wouldn't swallow the pills, he came out and helped."

"Did you notice anything about them?"

Flashbacks hit her at full force, each once causing her to blanch, to flinch, to want to run away, to retreat from the terrible thoughts. If only that were possible. "They wore masks. Were covered in black from head to toe."

"Is there anything you could remember? What did their voices sound like?"

She thought back before shrugging. "I almost thought one of them had an accent. He whispered. Very softly. I could hardly hear him. And

I couldn't tell you what kind of accent it was, only that it was slight."

"What about size?"

She shrugged again. "About average. But he was strong. I couldn't fight him."

"Any mannerisms or anything else that stood out?"

"No, I wish there were. I'm sorry."

"Don't apologize. You're doing fine. We checked the security footage, but someone erased it."

Erased it? Had she heard him correctly? The kind of knowledge and skills it would take someone to do that...

"What is it?" Mark leaned closer, looking entirely too fresh and composed after being up all night.

She was sure she must look like a wreck. Her hair felt stringy. The hospital gown was unflattering, to say the least. Not that any of that mattered. She wasn't trying to impress him. All she was focusing on right now was survival.

She pushed a hair behind her ear. "I'm a computer scientist. I do stuff like this for a living. It would take extensive knowledge to be able to hack into the hotel's security footage and erase it, especially so quickly after it happened." She blinked. "How long has it been?"

"It's been four hours, but I checked the footage out about thirty minutes after I found you."

She shook her head, trying to make sense of

everything as she lay in the sterile hospital room. "It's almost like there was someone outside in a van, monitoring the video feed. They would've had to erase the footage in real time and replace it with something prerecorded. It's very difficult."

Mark leaned closer, seeming more like a friend who was visiting than a detective out to nail her. "Do you know anyone with the capabilities of doing that?"

She ran through a list in her mind. She'd met a lot of really talented people at MIT. They were some of the best in the industry. Sure, they'd all done some stupid stuff in college—just because they could. But would any of them take it this far? Were any of them out to get her? She didn't think so.

"I don't know," she finally said. "I work alone. I don't have coworkers. But I suppose I've met a few people over the years. No one that I think would do this."

"Was your work…" He shifted as if uncomfortable. "Did it have any elements to it that might make someone dislike you or want to take you out?"

"I…" What could she say? This was always the part of her job that she was bad at. Lying. All those church lessons she'd learned growing up stained her thoughts and made her feel guilty. "I don't know. It's hard to say."

His eyes narrowed. "Why do I have a feeling there's something you're not telling me?"

She shrugged, trying to appear casual even though everything in her felt on alert. "It's just that my work is hard to describe. It's for clients who have confidentiality issues. I'm not always free to speak about these things."

His jaw flexed as he nodded, obviously unimpressed with her assessment. "We can subpoena your work, if we have to."

"You could…except my boss isn't answering his phone." She frowned and closed her eyes, her headache returning.

I could have died, she reminded herself. She'd come close. She was thankful to still be breathing.

"I've noticed that your boss has gone silent." He tilted his head. "Is that unusual?"

She nodded, remembering how Nicholas was usually very attentive, to the point where she'd wondered at one time if he was interested in her. *Day or night, give me a call. You need anything, I'm there. Anything. Do you understand?*

They'd had that conversation many, many times. Yet now when she needed him, he was nonexistent.

"It's very unusual."

Mark leveled his gaze with her. "We're going to need to talk to him."

She nodded. "I know. I'll give you his personal

cell number. And I'll keep trying. I only want to operate in the confines of my agreement."

"You do realize that your life is on the line."

"I do."

"Just to let you know, I put in a call to your husband's former commander, as well."

Her eyes widened with alarm. "Why would you do that? You think Nate is connected?"

"I just want to explore every possibility. I want to make sure this isn't in any way related to your husband's time in the service."

She nodded, everything feeling surreal. "Okay. Please, keep me updated."

"Of course." He stepped back as if realizing he'd gotten as much out of her as her current state would allow. "The hospital wants to keep you a little while longer for observation."

A shudder rippled through her. Staying there. *Alone.*

Her throat tightened at the thought. She'd always hated being alone, but even more so after what happened with Nate. Fear had overtaken her life for a long time, making her afraid to go out. Yet that same fear had pushed her away from people—people who could pull her out of her isolation. It had been a never-ending cycle.

Those fears hit her again. Would the men come back to finish what they'd started? Would they succeed the next time?

Before she realized what was happening, she

reached out and grabbed Mark's hand. She felt like she'd touched fire and instantly pulled back. "I'm sorry. I didn't mean to. It's just that…I don't know…those men."

"I understand, Laney."

"What if they…"

"I'll be stationed right outside or I'll have one of my men there. No one else will try to get to you. Not under my watch."

She let out the breath she'd been holding, her heart calming for a moment. "Thank you, Detective."

"Call me Mark."

She smiled. "Okay. Mark. Thank you again."

Mark leaned back in his chair, which was stationed right outside of Laney's hospital room. He'd found out that the pills she'd been forced to take were an antipsychotic, usually given to people with extreme mental disorders, and it acted as a sedative.

The amount she was given should have killed her. It would've claimed her life if he hadn't found her when he had. Thankfully, she would be okay, but it would take some time to recover.

Though he was nearly certain that she was a victim and not a suspect, he still wanted to keep his eyes wide-open. When his sister had been abducted, his stepfather had come up with a supposed alibi. He'd gone on air, crying about her disappearance and begging the public for their help. All along, he was behind her disappearance and murder.

Mark had dealt with trust issues ever since. Dating Chrystal hadn't helped anything. She'd only used him for his position at the police department. When Mark had confronted her about it, she'd fled and never looked back.

Something about Laney seemed different, though. She seemed so sincere. Not like someone wrapped up in pride. In winning. In always being right.

He couldn't pinpoint what it was exactly that gave him that impression. It was just the feeling he was left with when he was with her.

Eyes wide-open, he reminded himself.

Just then his phone rang. It was his partner. Mark had already been informed this morning that the FBI had been called in to help out with this case. As of now, Mark's only task was to keep an eye on Laney and see if she led him to any answers.

Though he wanted to be on the front lines, he understood his captain's position in assigning him to Laney. She seemed to trust him. They'd already developed some kind of bond. Besides, the FBI knew what they were doing. The most important thing here was getting Sarah back safe and sound.

"Did some digging," Jim said. "John Smith doesn't exist."

Mark didn't even flinch at the news. "I figured as much. How about a credit card?"

"He paid in cash."

Again, it wasn't really surprising. Whoever was behind this was smart and calculating. The plan had been thought out. "Does the woman at the front desk remember anything?"

"Apparently, the hotel clerk was talking on the phone to her boyfriend as he checked in and doesn't remember much of anything except her plans for tomorrow evening's date."

Mark resisted a sigh. Couldn't they catch a break? "What about the security footage from when the man checked in?"

"It was also erased."

"Why don't you check the footage from the gas station beside the hotel, as well. Maybe it will show a different angle."

"Will do. But whoever is behind this is really good. Knows what they're doing. Knows their way around technology. They've covered all their bases, so I doubt we'll find anything."

"That's what Laney said too."

"Laney?" Curiosity dripped from his voice. "Sounds personal."

Mark fought a frown, the sterile hospital hallway getting to him. "It's not personal. She is a software programmer, so she knows a little about this."

"So maybe one of her friends set all of this up. Erased the footage so *Laney* wouldn't look guilty. Maybe she's covering for them."

Mark's jaw hardened at Jim's implications. He knew his partner was right—and Mark had wondered the same things—but it bothered him to hear someone else voice their doubts about Laney out loud.

"If that's the case, then she set herself up to die tonight," Mark finally said. "Why would she do that? She had no guarantee that I'd go into the room when I did."

"How do you know she didn't take the pills when she heard you at the door? If you'd come to her room in the morning, maybe she would have taken them then."

Mark shook his head, readying to vehemently deny his claim. He drew in a deep breath in an effort to calm himself down first. Getting prickly wouldn't do anyone any good. "That's one theory, I suppose. But I don't buy it. I saw her. She's scared. Besides, there were footprints."

"One member of the cleaning staff is a man. It could have been his. We're testing the prints against his now."

He closed his eyes and let his head fall back against the wall in pure exhaustion. This case was taking everything out of him and it was no-where near being over yet. "Did you discover anything else?"

"No one saw anything—no men in black creep-ing around. It was the middle of the night. Most people were sleeping. I'll keep asking around and see if I can find out anything else. Don't hold your breath, though. What's next for you?"

"Captain said to keep an eye on Laney. I plan on doing that. I'm not letting her leave my sight, not until I know who's behind all of this."

"Glad it's you and not me. Have fun."

Mark forced his eyes open and ran a hand over his face. "Yeah, yeah, I hear you."

"Oh, and by the way, did you say you talked to the commander of the SEAL team Nate Ryan was a part of?"

"That's right. Commander Rankin. He said there hadn't been any threats on Nate Ryan's SEAL team in a couple of years. He said if any-thing comes to his attention, he'll let us know."

"Good to know. I just wanted to double-check."

He hung up and stared off into the distance a moment as a woman pushed a food cart toward rooms at the end of the hallway.

He had no leads. No clues. No nothing.

The person behind this was really good.

And what about that accent Laney had men-tioned hearing on one of the men? How did that fit into this whole mystery?

This whole mystery kept getting more confusing by the moment.

Laney had begged the doctor to let her go and finally, at 10:00 a.m., he had. Someone had stopped by with her personal belongings from the hotel, which meant she had clean clothes as well as her purse. The effects of the drug seemed to have worn off, and she was feeling much more clearheaded.

Self-consciously, she pushed a hair behind her ear when she spotted Mark outside her door. Her cheeks flushed, the reaction surprising once again. What was that? Relief? Excitement? Gratefulness?

He didn't look quite as put together as he had yesterday, but he still looked awfully good, all things considered. He must have swung by his home at some point because he wore a gray henley, jeans, boots and his black leather jacket. The look was…it was nice.

She noticed all this more as an observation—it had nothing to do with an interest in him. At least, that's what she told herself. Besides, an attraction to the man was futile. He thought she was guilty. At least, he thought there was a possibility she was guilty.

He stood, an unreadable expression on his face. "Laney. How are you feeling?"

"Better than yesterday. Thank you for standing guard out here."

"No problem. I'm just glad you haven't had any more trouble. You ready to go?"

"I don't even know where to tell you to take me," she muttered, hating that he was seeing her in her weakness. But she couldn't lie. She had no one except her in-laws, but they were both in poor health and lived six hours away. She couldn't leave the state, as per orders of the police since she was their number-one suspect.

"Your parents? A sister or brother?"

"My dad is unknown. My mom went through a wild period of partying and drug addiction. She gave custody of me over to my grandmother when I was less than a year old and then she disappeared. My grandma died six years ago, and I have no brothers or sisters—that I know of, at least."

"I see."

She raised a hand to halt his thoughts. "Don't feel sorry for me. It's just life. You do what you have to do to get by."

"Understood." He paused a moment. "Speaking of which, I have a friend you could probably stay with."

Her heart warmed for some unknown reason at his offer. "I couldn't ask that."

Compassion made his eyes look soft and kind. "You didn't. I'm offering. He and his wife are nice. They don't have any kids. And he's a former cop."

She wanted to argue, but she knew she was desperate and out of options. She couldn't stomach the thought of staying at a hotel again—not after what had happened. She wasn't sure there was anywhere she'd really feel safe. Not in a hotel surrounded by people. Not in a cabin by herself.

Really, the only scenario where she might feel safe would be with Nate, and Nate was no longer here. That meant her entrenching fear was something she was going to have to learn to live with.

"Thank you. That's really kind of you. I assume you'll be leaving me there so you can investigate." The question felt awkward as it came out of her mouth. But the thought of being stranded at a stranger's house and being forced to chitchat while so much was on the line made her uncomfortable.

She'd never been a whiz in social situations. She preferred small groups of close friends. Of course, she'd recently secluded herself from the joy of those relationships lately too.

He frowned. "I'll probably have another officer wait outside to keep an eye on you. I need to get a few hours of shut-eye."

Guilt flashed through her. "I'm sorry. I should have never asked you to stay last night. It was selfish of me. The drugs…they were messing with my mind. Without them, I would have never imposed like that."

"I didn't mind. What you went through was traumatic. I'll need to get your official statement sometime for a police report."

They started walking down the hallway. Laney was grateful for his graciousness. Not everyone would be as kind.

"Any word on Sarah?" she asked.

He shook his head. "No. Nothing yet. Everything's gone quiet. We're waiting to hear from the kidnappers again."

Her bottom lip quivered as she thought about her neighbor. "I hope she's okay. I hate to think about her being scared right now. I've been scared. I've lived in fear, for that matter. It's not a fun place to be."

"You're right. It's no way to live. Believe me— the police are doing everything they can to help find her."

"No more ransom calls?"

He shook his head. "No, not yet."

"Why not?" she muttered, slowing her steps. Money had to be the end result…right? Wasn't it always? She would think the men behind this would be anxious to get paid and move on.

"What was that?"

She snapped her head toward Mark. "Why no ransom? Isn't that usually what kidnappers do? They want money. Does Sol even have that much money?"

"He works at an accounting firm, correct?"

She nodded. "That's right. I've never had the impression that he's rich. I mean, what other reason do people kidnap if not for money? For leverage maybe?"

"Generally it happens in custody disputes. Random kidnappings by strangers are unusual. And you're right—money is usually involved."

"It just doesn't make any sense to me." Her cheeks warmed when she realized he was looking at her. She shoved a hair behind her ear. "What?"

"Either you're a really good actor or you really aren't involved in this."

"I'm not involved. I'll prove it to you."

His eyebrows shot up. "What's that mean? You're not planning on getting mixed up in this, are you?"

"Planning on it? I'm already mixed up and not by my own choice. No one else is going to take the time to prove my innocence. That's my job."

"You don't know who you could be messing with, Laney. They already tried to kill you once. The best thing you can do is find a good lawyer."

"I can't sit around and do nothing. In fact, if you take me to my car, I'll drive to your friend's house. At least then I'll have some transportation."

"I don't think that's a good idea."

At that moment, Mark's phone rang and he put it to his ear. After a series of grunts, Laney knew it couldn't be good news. When he hit End, his expression was grim.

"Laney, we won't be getting your car."

"Why's that?"

His gaze was full of compassion. "Your house was set on fire. Your car was destroyed during the blaze. I'm so sorry."

EIGHT

Laney grabbed the wall before she collapsed on the ground. Her house? On fire?

Mark grasped her elbow and lowered her into a chair. She buckled there, unable to hold herself up any longer.

Why? Why is all this happening?

Mark kneeled beside her. His eyebrows were knit together, as if he were ready to call a doctor if he saw any signs she needed one. His concern appeared genuine and sincere enough that her heart momentarily warmed.

"You okay?" he asked.

She nodded. Her whole world had collapsed in a matter of hours. That's what it felt like, at least. "I guess. I don't know what to think or how to feel right now."

He gave her a few minutes of silence to process the information, time that she appreciated. She couldn't handle rapid-fire questions right now. Her house had burned down. Her house. Everything she had was gone. Soon her future would also vanish if she didn't find some answers.

"What happened?" she finally asked.

Mark lowered himself into the vinyl chair beside her and turned toward her, watching each of her movements carefully. "Investigators are still trying to figure it out. They're not sure yet. Maybe an electrical fire."

She shook her head, his words causing some kind of mental backlash. "This was no accident."

His eyes narrowed in thought. "You think someone purposely set your house on fire? Just like they threw that bottle bomb earlier? Like someone's trying to make some kind of statement?"

Laney stared at the people coming and going around her, some rushing toward rooms, others rushing to get home. Others dragged their feet and looked somber. Life was often a reflection of both of those urges: anxious for tomorrow yet hesitant to let go of today.

Mark had asked her a question. Why would someone set her house on fire? "Exactly," she finally said. "Or someone wants to let me know they're not done trying to ruin my life."

He twisted his head, not looking convinced. "That's pretty dramatic, isn't it?"

"So is accusing someone of kidnapping."

Mark let out his breath and leaned into his chair. "I can't argue with that."

At least they could both agree on one thing. It was a start. But Laney still had a lot to figure out. The handsome detective seemed to be intent on keeping an eye on her every move. How would she find answers if he was always close?

On the other hand, how was she going to survive another day if he left her?

The conundrum pulled her in two directions and made her feel light-headed.

"How about if we swing you by your house? Do you feel up to it?"

She nodded, though she was feeling utterly weak and at a loss. But she couldn't give up. She had no choice but to continue pressing forward.

Mark helped her up to her feet. She wanted to reject his assistance, but she knew she might collapse again if she tried to stand on her own. He kept a hand on her elbow as they made their way toward the hospital exit. She couldn't deny the fact that his touch made her blood feel warm.

The thought caused her cheeks to heat. She couldn't be attracted to the detective. She was just giving him some kind of hero worship. That had to be it. She hadn't been attracted to anyone since Nate, and the thought made her feel off balance.

She had more important things to think about.

Everything was lost, she realized as reality continued to sink in. It wasn't the majority of the material possessions that concerned her. She could replace much of that.

It was the sentimental she mourned for. The photos. Her wedding ring. Mementos from her time with Nate. Those were things she could never get back again.

A little cry escaped.

"I'm sorry, Laney," Mark murmured as they stepped outside and bright morning sunlight warmed her otherwise frigid skin.

It was then she noticed that a tear had slid down her cheek. "All of my memories of Nate were there. Now they're…they're all gone."

He squeezed her elbow, maneuvering her between cars pulling toward the entrance. "Maybe the damage isn't as bad as we think."

"I just don't understand why someone would do this to me."

Mark said nothing. She didn't even care what he was thinking. Maybe he still wondered if she was guilty. Let him think whatever he wanted. She knew the truth. She'd find evidence to prove it.

They made it to Mark's car, he helped her to the passenger door, and a few minutes later they were headed down the road.

There was no way she could fully comprehend what had happened. If she did, she might go into shock. Instead, she tried to swallow the news piece by piece.

Someone kidnapped Sarah and set Laney up to look guilty.

Someone tried to kill Laney and set it up to look like she killed herself.

Someone set her house on fire… What were they setting it up to look like this time? Obviously, Laney couldn't be blamed. She'd been in the hospital all night, and Mark had been on guard outside of her room.

Was she in for another whammy when she arrived at her property, though? She didn't even know how to brace herself for it. Would they find some way to point this all back at her? To make it sound like she'd somehow arranged it all?

She pulled her sweatshirt closer. The day was cold, and even the windows felt like ice and carried waves of coolness all the way to her seat in the car. The glass frosted up in the frigid temperatures, and gray overcast sky only added to the effect.

The weather seemed to perfectly fit her life right now, as if God Himself knew how she was feeling and sympathized.

God, I need someone's help right now. You're the God of comfort. Will You give me some peace? Please?

"I thought I'd let you know that we're running a license plate on a car from the gas station parking lot last night." Mark's voice cut into her thoughts.

"What was that?" Why did a car from a gas station matter?

"This was the station located right next to the

hotel. We thought maybe someone had parked there, trying to avoid the cameras in the hotel parking lot. We were right."

"That's good news."

"We believe the car may contain the two men who attacked you last night. We're hoping to get a hit. Right now, we know that it's a rental, so we're trying to track down whoever signed the paperwork."

"Let me guess—John Smith?"

He said nothing.

"I'd also guess that all of the security footage from the car rental company disappeared," she continued. She had to think like a criminal in her line of work in order to anticipate what they might do next. These guys behind this were smart. Too smart.

"We're still working on it. At least the gas station footage proves that there were two men. They've covered up any other evidence."

She nodded, wishing she didn't feel so bleak. "Thank you."

As soon as the words left her lips, Mark pulled to a stop in front of her house. Her bottom lip dropped open at the scene. Charred timbers remained where the roof once was. The bricks, once red, were now black and crumbling. Windows had busted. The vinyl siding near the pitch of the roof was melted and like a blob.

Puddles remained on the lawn from where, no

doubt, firefighters had battled to put out the blaze. Two trucks were still catty-corner on the street, and neighbors had gathered around to observe the destruction. Were they glad to see someone accused of the things she'd been accused of suffering?

Laney knew without talking to the fire chief that everything was destroyed, and grief washed through her at the thought.

She was all alone with no one to care for her and nothing in her name. Everything had been stripped away. The thought momentarily made her want to give up.

But she knew she couldn't. She had to believe that there was something more out there for her.

God had always provided for her, even in the toughest times. He wouldn't leave her now in the middle of this battle.

She couldn't lose hope. But it was going to be an uphill struggle.

Mark wished he could do something to comfort Laney. He'd prayed for her last night. He'd also prayed for Sarah and for Sol. For this whole situation. He prayed over every case he worked, knowing that leaving it in the Lord's hands was the best solution to all of his problems.

Still, he wished there weren't professional boundaries in place because Laney looked like she desperately needed a hug. She stood on what used to be her front lawn, her arms wrapped over her chest, and her face pale with the effects of loss and stress.

He remained at a distance—close enough to keep an eye on her, but far enough away to finish up his conversation with the fire chief. He hadn't learned anything new—he knew he wouldn't. There would have to be an investigation first.

He glanced at Laney again. It was obvious she was trying to be strong, but she gave her emotions away. Occasionally when she looked at her house—at the remains of it—her chin trembled, belying the storm going on inside. Anyone would have that reaction after seeing their house destroyed. A certain form of grief came with losing everything you owned.

He couldn't just abandon the woman. "How about if I take you to my friend's house—the one I mentioned earlier?"

She glanced at him, surprise echoing through her gaze, before she sucked in a deep breath. Courage seeming to fill her with the motion and she gave a resolute shake of the head. "No. I need to go to the bank. And then I have a few other stops to make."

"The bank?"

"I have some money in my safe-deposit box. Cash. It will be enough that I can rent a car and maybe buy some clothes until all of this blows over."

Something twisted in his gut, an unreasonable

sense of loyalty to the woman that included a myriad of worries over her going out on her own. "And then what will do you?"

She blinked several times before meeting his gaze. "You really want to know?"

He nodded. Did he ever. "I do."

"I'm going to Fro Yo Yo."

He squinted, uncertain if he'd heard her correctly. "What?"

She let out a sigh and ran a hand through her hair. "Sarah's friend works at the frozen yogurt shop on weekends. I want to talk to him."

At least that made more sense, and he knew it wasn't the drugs still gripping her mind. "I'll take you."

She looked up at him, her eyes as round as saucers and utterly apologetic. "I'm sure you need to get rest."

He was tired, but his adrenaline was keeping him going. There was too much at stake to rest. "I don't mind. Especially with everything going on. Your life…it's in danger."

"I'm sure your captain has other things for you to do besides babysit me."

She had no idea. "He'll be fine with it. Besides, I want answers about Sarah just as much as anyone. There's already been a task force started, and the feds are moving in."

She crossed her arms, surprisingly calm. Or was it resigned? He wasn't sure.

"If you insist," she said. "I gave you an out, though."

Honestly, he wasn't sure if Laney could survive out there on her own right now. She looked tired, and the drugs were probably still weaning from her system. If she came face-to-face with a killer again, she might not survive next time.

As she requested, he took her to the bank and then stopped briefly at a department store. She emerged wearing clean clothes and with her hair combed.

"No one will take me seriously looking like I did back there," she quickly explained. "Looking good isn't my top priority, but I don't want to scare anyone away."

He didn't think she would have scared anyone away. Even wearing old hospital clothes and with her hair pulled into a sloppy ponytail, she still looked lovely. Not many people could manage that, but Laney had a natural beauty that wasn't defined by her clothes and makeup. But he didn't tell her that.

Where had that thought come from? Mark shook his head, trying to push it aside. He needed to stay focused here. She wanted to talk to Sarah's friend. Mark thought that was a great idea. He was also interested in hearing what this friend had to say. Jim was in the process of interviewing everyone who knew Sarah, but Mark had been absent from those talks.

The frozen yogurt shop wasn't far away—less than five minutes. Laney rubbed her hands against her pants before opening the car door.

"You ready for this?" he asked.

She sucked in a breath before nodding. "I need answers. Literally. Without them, I could lose everything."

"Let's go see what we can find out then."

They climbed out and skirted around some scaffolding out at the front of the shop—left by the crew painting the header, it appeared—in order to reach the frozen yogurt establishment. They stepped inside the storefront, and a blast of cool air hit their already frigid skin.

The place was painted a bright pink and lime green, and no one was inside except a tall, lanky teenage boy with shaggy dark hair and a thin, barely there mustache. It was so cold outside that most people weren't flocking to the shop for a cool treat.

The teen offered a welcoming smile as he wiped down the countertop near the register. "Welcome to Fro Yo Yo."

"Are you Danny?" Laney asked as she approached the counter.

The boy's smile slipped. "I am. Do I know you?"

Laney shook her head. "No, not really. But I was a friend of Sarah's. I *am* a friend of Sarah's."

Danny's eyes noticeably widened with fear and

worry. "Is there an update? Did they find her? Is she okay?"

Laney put her hand over his. "No. I'm sorry. I wish I had an update, that I had good news. But I'm still looking for answers."

He jerked his hand away and pulled back. "Are you...are you her neighbor? The one everyone is accusing of snatching her?"

His gaze went to Mark's as the boy tried to put everything together.

"I didn't take Sarah," Laney insisted, a plea to her voice. "I think of her like a daughter. In fact, I'm trying to find her."

"I'm Detective Mark James." Mark flashed his badge, knowing he needed to step in, in order to establish some trust. "We're just here to ask questions."

That pronouncement seemed to ease the teen's anxiety. He sucked in a deep breath and nodded slowly, beginning to wipe the counter again but this time much more methodically. "What do you want to know? I don't know anything. I wish I did."

"We're just trying to find some answers," Mark said.

"I want to help. I didn't sleep at all last night. I kept thinking about what Sarah might be going through." He hung his head as if his burdens were too heavy to bear.

"It's okay, Danny." Laney's voice took on a

nurturing tone as she leaned toward the boy. "I just wanted to know if Sarah had been acting strangely in the days before she disappeared. Did she say anything that caused you any alarm?"

Danny shook his head. "No. Nothing. It seemed like usual, I guess. 'Usual' being that she was miserable."

Mark glanced at Laney and saw her eyes twitch with concern and surprise.

"What do you mean?" she asked.

Danny shrugged. "Look, I know a lot of my friends have issues with their parents. We're teens. We're rebellious and trying to take the world by storm while our parents want us to stay their babies forever. I get that. But she was counting down the days until she was old enough to move out."

"I knew she wasn't happy, but did she tell you why?"

He shrugged and let out a heavy sigh. "I don't know. She said her dad was acting erratically. I couldn't tell you how or why. He always acted like that to me. He never liked me, and I wasn't allowed to go to her house. He said I was a bad influence."

"She didn't say how he was acting erratically?" Mark asked.

"Not really. Just that his job was stressful, and she had to always walk on eggshells. She felt smothered by him."

A theory desperately wanted to emerge from

the depths of Mark's mind. What was it? It floated just below the surface, begging for his attention. And it didn't have anything to do with this conversation. It was a thought that had been forming in his subconscious all day. Some kind of connection that he needed to make, a theory he needed to explore.

It was Laney's job, he realized.

Something about it bugged him…or maybe it intrigued him. Someone obviously wanted to drag Laney into this. Did what she does for a living have some kind of strange connection between her career and Sarah's disappearance?

He decided not to bring it up yet. He wanted to chew on the theory for a while first.

"When was the last time you heard from her?" Laney asked.

"The morning she disappeared. Was that just yesterday? It seems like so long ago already. She was at school but then got a text and said she had to leave."

"Did she say where she was going?" Mark continued.

"To meet you." He leveled his gaze with Laney.

She froze, her entire body looking tense. "I didn't send that text."

"She thought you did," Danny said. "There are very few people she would have left school for, especially knowing how mad her father would be. Grades and school are very important to him."

So the person behind all of this knew that Laney had influence in Sarah's life. Interesting. "Anything else?"

The boy thought for a moment before shrugging. "She did mention something about possibly having to move soon. She was even thinking about trying to get some kind of special legal provision that would let her stay here until she graduated. She didn't want to move."

"Move where?" Laney looked and sounded honestly perplexed at the possibility.

"She didn't say. She only mentioned something about a job possibility for her father that would take them out of this area."

"Thank you for your help," Mark said, absorbing the new information.

As they stepped outside, his muscles tightened. He'd finely trained his instincts for danger. And right now, it felt imminent.

He scanned the parking lot.

"What is it?" Laney asked, tensing along with him.

"I don't know."

He didn't see anything out of the ordinary. Cars drove past in the distance. A bird squawked overhead. Something scraped against the roof— maybe one of the construction workers above.

So what was causing his senses to go on alert? Was someone watching them?

Maybe they should get to the car. The more quickly, the better. Nowhere felt safe at the moment.

He put his hand on Laney's back, ready to quickly escort her across the parking lot. He'd keep his eyes open for any approaching vehicles or lurking shadows as they went.

Just as they stepped onto the asphalt, he heard another footstep above him. Then a crack.

The next moment, the scaffolding beside them crashed. Tools and buckets torpedoed toward them. Wooden boards slid from their holders. Metal bars toppled.

The weight of everything could be devastating on a human body.

Mark dove toward Laney, desperate to keep her safe.

But he feared he was too late.

NINE

Laney looked up and saw all the equipment tumbling toward her. She froze with fear as a sharp drill headed toward her face.

"Watch out!" Mark shouted.

Before she could react, Mark covered her as he dove toward the sidewalk. He twisted himself around, padding her fall and shielding her from the shrapnel from the scaffolding at the same time.

She squeezed her eyes shut, waiting to feel the pain of being punctuated, scraped, cut. She anticipated hearing Mark groan as the weight of the boards and metal trapped him.

Finally, the noise stopped. The avalanche was over and all she could hear now was her heart pounding in her ears.

Was she okay? Or had they been buried? Was Mark okay?

The questions thundered through her head, yet she remained frozen.

Mark spoke before she could. "Laney?"

She realized her eyes were squeezed shut. Finally, she forced herself to look around. She appeared to be unharmed—there was no blood or mangled bones or obvious signs of injury.

By some act of God, they'd come through that without a scratch. Well, maybe a few scratches and bruises, but far less than she thought they'd have. Some of the heavy equipment could have put them out of commission.

She looked up and realized that Mark was practically on top of her. She pulled in a breath at the realization. It wasn't so much his physical closeness—it was the fact that she was attracted to him. That she could see the slivers of gray in his blue eyes. That she could smell his piney cologne. That she could feel his heart beating against hers.

All of it left her feeling discombobulated. Breathless. Both warm with pleasure and cold with fear.

"Laney?" Mark repeated.

"I'm okay." Her voice sounded shaky, and she hoped Mark would assume the reaction was because of the danger they'd just faced, not at his nearness. "You?"

He pushed himself up, bits of plaster falling from his shoulders. "Yeah, I'm fine."

As he moved, Laney viewed the wreckage. A huge pile of rubble lay where they had both been standing. They would have been buried. One of those poles could have easily pierced them. Killed them, for that matter.

It was even worse than she'd imagined.

"What happened?" she muttered, her bones aching with each movement.

"I'm not sure, but that wasn't a coincidence." He stood and helped her to her feet. His eyes looked dark and stormy as he looked off into the distance. "Stay here."

He darted into the parking lot and looked toward the roof. As he did so, the crowd began gathering, gawking at the damage. Danny was one of the first ones out.

"Are you okay?" he asked, running up to her.

She nodded, trying to ignore the tremble in her hands. "Somehow I can answer that with a yes."

"Thank God. I heard the crash after you guys left, and I thought the worst."

She smiled as his words. "That's right. Thank God."

He looked at the pile of metal and wood and buckets. "The workers must have just left for a break. They've been out there all week. I can't believe they would leave their job site unsecure like that."

Even as Danny talked, Laney's gaze followed Mark. He'd darted around to the back of the building. What was going on? Had someone really done that on purpose? That was Mark's theory, she realized.

It was another attempt on her life, staged to look like an accident.

Someone wanted to make sure it looked like she'd died either at her own hands or by coincidence. It was becoming exceedingly clear that if she didn't find answers, she might not make it another day.

A chill washed through her at the thought.

Just as Mark emerged from the back of the building, a police car pulled up. Mark talked to the officer for several minutes while Danny stayed with her. The rest of the crowds seemed to dissipate, their curiosity satisfied.

Finally Mark made his way toward her again. "Whoever did this is gone."

"You really think someone did this on purpose?" She knew the truth but she wanted to hear him say it.

He nodded, his gaze flickering to the mess around them. The crew returned and talked to the police officer. Even from where Laney stood, she could hear the construction workers denying their involvement, claiming they left the area secure.

"I have no doubt that this was on purpose," Mark said. "Someone must have waited until we were done talking to Danny and tried to make it look like an accident. They must have followed us here. Maybe they've been following us all day, for that matter.

"But why?"

He took her elbow and led her away from the craziness of the shopping center. "I wish I knew. Let's get out of here and talk. I've already given my statement. Officer Payson will contact us if he has more questions."

Mark didn't let go of her until they were in his car. Even then, his gaze was hard as he continuously scanned around them. He cranked the engine and turned on the heat to stave away the cold.

"Did you see anyone?" she finally asked, desperate to make sense of things. Feeling like she'd lived enough over the past twenty-four hours to fill a whole year instead of a day.

Mark shook his head, his expression still hard as he stared out the front windshield. "No, but I want to be certain that no one tries something again. There's too much at stake here."

"Just me."

"Like I said, there's too much."

Her cheeks warmed before she realized the error of her statement. There was definitely more at stake than just her. Sarah was at stake. It appeared that Mark's life was also on the line. The situation continued to spiral into one giant disaster.

But Mark had said her life alone was worth the risk. Was he being sincere? His words caused something to shift and flutter inside her.

No man had had this effect on her since Nate,

and she didn't want that to change. She knew she'd never find someone else like her husband. She'd be asking for too much to even whisper the thought, to even begin to hope that.

No, Nate had been strong and loyal and patient...everything she could want in a man. Not perfect, but no one was. Finding a man like Nate had been a once-in-a-lifetime opportunity.

"Whoever is behind this is obviously a tech genius, Laney. They were able to hack in to your phone and make it look like you sent a message to Sarah. They opened a bank account in your name, stopped the check you sent en route, and deposited it into the new account. They gained control of the security cameras at the hotel. None of that is a small feat."

She sucked on her bottom lip a moment, unable to deny his words. "I agree. Someone is brilliant at these things."

"This person either has a partner or he's willing to go the extra mile to attack you."

"I agree."

His eyes narrowed. "You work for a tech company, correct?"

She nodded, her thoughts slowing to a crawl. "That's right."

"What if someone at your work is behind this?"

The idea made her thoughts move from a slow crawl to a grinding halt. "Why would they be?"

"You tell me."

She tried to remain expressionless, tried not to show too much. If only she could tell him the truth—the whole truth. But she'd taken an oath that she couldn't break. "I have no enemies there. It's like I said, I work alone and have only one contact—my boss."

He pulled out his phone. "I want to call him."

Her heart began racing again. She and Nicholas had gone over that plan. They had a cover organization that would answer. They even had a physical office in case people—relatives usually—stopped by.

Mark would think he was calling CybCorp. A receptionist should answer and confirm that she was an employee.

She'd only tried to call Nicholas herself, and she still felt unsettled that he wasn't answering.

"Of course." Her voice caught.

She gave Mark Nicholas's number, and he dialed. A moment later, he lowered the phone. "No one answered."

She pushed a hair behind her ear. Sorrow lingered in her voice. "He hasn't answered for me, either."

Mark narrowed his eyes, shifting to face her better. "Don't you find that unusual?"

"I do. But I don't know what to do about it. Maybe he took a vacation or became ill. It isn't like him not to answer."

"There's no other number you can call?"

She shook her head. "No, I wish there were. But I've never needed any other numbers. It might sound far-fetched, but it's the truth."

He started tapping away on his phone, acting like he was on a mission.

"What are you doing?" she asked, her curiosity peaked.

"I'm looking to see if there are any other numbers I can call."

The tension in her gut grew. "I see."

"Aha," he finally said. "Here's one for Cyb-Corp. Let's see if I can get an answer now."

She held her breath, waiting to see how everything would play out. Would her cover be blown? Why wasn't her boss responding? Didn't he realize how suspicious that made her look?

Mark pulled the phone away and frowned. "There's a message saying the number has been disconnected." He stared at her, long and hard until she cringed.

"I don't know what you're implying, but I can assure you they exist. They've been writing me a paycheck for the past year."

"Do you have an address?" he asked.

"Of course. Would you like it?"

"As a matter of fact, I would. I'm going to have some of my guys check it out."

"You still think I'm behind this?" After everything he'd seen and experienced with her, how could he believe that? The only way it was possible was if she had a death wish for herself. Any relief she'd experienced had been mistaken. Mark wasn't on her side.

His gaze remained sharp. "I think you're connected somehow. I don't know in what way yet."

"If someone I work with is trying to kill me, why kidnap Sarah? What does she have to do with any of this? What does she have to do with me?"

"I have no idea. I'm only asking questions at this point."

Her thoughts raced. "What about Sarah's dad? Danny said he'd been acting strange lately. Maybe he knows something. Maybe he's being targeted."

"Most teens think their parents are strange. Even Danny said so."

"But he was acting *suspiciously* strange. And moving for another job? I hadn't heard about that."

"So you think Sarah staged this herself so she wouldn't have to leave the area?"

Laney's mouth dropped open. "What? No. That's not what I said. She's smarter than that. Maybe she would have just left. But she wouldn't have staged something so dramatic."

"Maybe if she was desperate. I've seen desperate people do things no one ever suspected they would do."

"Well, she wasn't like that. You don't know her." She crossed her arms, hating how upset she felt but unable to shake it. How dare Mark accuse Sarah of being behind this. And what would she do when the truth came out about her work? Would her cover be revealed?

It was best if she put as much distance between herself and this man as possible. Thinking she could trust him might be her biggest mistake. Whatever bond she'd felt with him was short-lived.

"Could you drop me off somewhere I can rent a car?"

He stared at her a moment, his expression un-readable. "Is that really what you want?"

She nodded, surprisingly sad about the separation she knew she needed to put between herself and the man who'd been her protector for the last twenty-four hours. "Yes, I'm sure. You don't have to babysit me anymore."

"I think this is a bad idea," he muttered. "Just for the record."

"You have a kidnapper to catch. That's way more important than me."

He rubbed his jaw, like he wanted to say more. But he didn't.

Instead, he pulled up to a car rental agency a couple of blocks away.

Her throat clenched as she climbed out. She had a feeling this wouldn't be the last time she saw the detective. But she dreaded to think what might bring them together for their next encounter. More accusations? Another attempt on her life?

Not if she found Sarah first.

"Thanks again," she murmured.

"Take care of yourself, Laney. Be careful."

Mark pulled onto a side street and waited for Laney to emerge from the car rental agency. She did ten minutes later, driving a light blue sedan. She headed toward downtown Richmond.

What was she going to do? Though his body longed for rest, his mind was alert. Whatever was going on here was dangerous and twisted at the same time.

He'd never seen so many blatant attempts on someone's life and he was convinced the worst was yet to come. He needed to keep an eye on Laney—both because the captain had told him to and because she reminded him of an innocent doe caught in a hunter's crosshairs. She wasn't equipped to handle situations like these. Not on her own.

Slowly, he pulled out behind her, making sure he put enough distance between her and himself so she wouldn't catch wind of his presence. He wanted to find out what she was hiding.

She drove several miles around the outskirts of Richmond before pausing in front of Allegra Accounting. Allegra Accounting? What in the world was she doing here? Getting financial advice?

He stayed back, watching as she put the car in Park. It almost appeared she was poised to get out when someone exited the building.

Mark sucked in a breath. Sol Novak.

Sol worked there? So why had Laney come?

He braced himself for whatever was about to play out. A confrontation? A secret meeting? He had no idea.

Instead of getting out and talking to him, Laney remained in the car.

Sol hurried across the parking lot, his overcoat flapping in the wind. His gaze skittered around him each step. It was almost like he knew he was being watched.

Did the FBI know what he was doing?

And why was Sol back at work already? Some people liked to stay busy in order to keep their minds occupied in the face of tragedy. But his daughter had just disappeared yesterday. And it was a weekend, at that.

Something wasn't adding up, and he could feel danger looming on the horizon.

As Sol climbed into his own vehicle and pulled out, Laney began following behind him.

Interesting.

Five minutes later, Sol stopped at a park near downtown Richmond. After climbing out with a cup of coffee in hand, he walked toward a bench that faced the lake at the center of the busy grounds.

What was he doing there? Things kept getting stranger and stranger. The tension in Mark grew by the minute.

Laney continued to lie low, remaining in her car with her eyes riveted on Sol. Mark had parked at the perfect position to keep an eye on both of them.

Sol walked to a bench and sat for a minute watching people pass him on the lakeside trail. Several people passed. Some were speed walking on their lunch breaks. Others were walking dogs. Moms chased young children. Two men on bikes breezed past.

He saw the man reach into his coat pocket and pull out a thin manila envelope. He reached beneath the bench, pressed it there, and then subtly looked around. Not missing a beat, Sol stood, straightened his jacket and started back to his car.

What had just happened? Had he just made a drop of some kind? Was he leaving money for the kidnappers? The package didn't seem big enough for any kind of sizable amount of cash.

Mark waited for Sol to climb back into his car. His gaze flickered to Laney. She remained in her car, but she looked poised to move. She wanted to see what was in that package too.

Before either of them could get out, a brunette wearing a scarf and glasses appeared on the opposite side of the walkway, headed toward the bench Sol had vacated and sat down.

Mark studied her for a moment. Something about her seemed familiar.

She looked like Laney he realized.

Could this woman somehow be involved in Sarah's abduction? Did a neighbor mistake her for Laney since their features were similar?

More so, was she picking up some kind of ransom from Sol? Where were the police right now? The feds should know about this.

He got on his phone and called for backup, wishing he'd done so five minutes ago.

The woman reached beneath the bench, grabbed the package and stood.

He couldn't let her get away yet. He couldn't be everywhere at once. If she hopped into a vehicle, then he'd lose her on foot.

He tried to be patient, waiting for the right moment to act.

He didn't care about Laney spotting him at that point. Someone inexperienced like Laney could mess this all up, though.

The woman backed from the parking space and began to exit the area.

As he pulled out to follow the woman, Laney did the same. This was a disaster waiting to happen. But there was no way to stop her now. Attempting to would only alert the brunette that she was being followed.

The woman pulled out onto the main highway. As soon as she did, she rapidly accelerated.

An impending feeling of doom pressed on his shoulders. This was going to end badly. And there was little he could do to stop it.

In front of him, Laney sped toward an inter-section. The light turned yellow. She kept going forward.

He heard the screeching of tires seconds before he saw a car ram right into Laney's door.

TEN

Laney felt her world spin again. Everything blurred around her. Her body and mind didn't move together. Everything seemed fast, yet in slow motion.

She blinked, trying to make sense of the moment.

Smoke rose from the hood of her rental. Shattered glass glimmered around her, falling out of her hair even. The smell of something hot and burning hit her nose. She coughed as the powder from the air bag aspirated into her lungs.

Shouts sounded around her. Vehicles squealed as they scrambled to avoid her. People appeared in the street, some to gawk, others rushing to help.

She let her head fall to the side. A black truck had hit her. The impact had pushed the vehicle away from the point of the collision and away from her door. She had the impression that her sedan had received the bulk of the damage.

She blinked again and saw the driver, sitting

in his truck, staring at her. Was he in shock? Was he okay?

He didn't move yet his eyes were open. Was he even alive?

Events began replaying in her mind. She'd been chasing the brunette from the park. The light had been yellow when she went through…right?

Trembles overtook her muscles. Panic seized her thoughts.

In a blur, she saw Mark appear at her door. "Laney?"

She tried to respond but couldn't. Her lips wouldn't cooperate.

Using his coat, he pushed away shards of glass atop her window, removing the last of the broken pieces. He mumbled something, probably assurances.

Laney willed her lips to move. Finally something indiscernible escaped. More of a moan than words.

All at once, words tumbled from her mouth, sounding like nonsense until finally, "Sol… woman…followed."

Mark reached into the car and unclasped her seat belt. "We'll talk about that later. Right now we have to get you out of this car. Can you move?"

Could she? She tried to pull her leg up from beneath the dashboard. Yes—it worked. She appeared to be in one piece and totally functional. Thank God!

"Yes," she whispered.

Mark reached his arms beneath her and lifted her. Gently, he brought her through the window and out of the car. His strong arms made him seem like a rock beneath her, like a source of strength worth holding on to. Her head flopped onto his chest.

He carried her across the street and laid her on the sidewalk, away from her battered car. Away from the gawking crowds. Away from the nightmare that surrounded her. As she felt the sidewalk beneath her, everything tilted around her.

Her body ached. Her head throbbed. But she was alive.

That meant that Mark could chase after the woman in the car before it was too late. Before their one lead got away.

"You've got to go after that woman..." She pointed to the car she'd been following. It was long gone. Time had seemed fluid, and she couldn't even guess how many minutes had passed. One? Five? Thirty?

Mark knelt beside her, studying her face. "Other officers are in pursuit. I've got the license plate. You don't worry about that."

She pushed herself up, ignoring her wobbling head. Ignoring the stares of those around her. Trying to pinpoint the facts that tugged at her consciousness. What was it that begged to get her attention? She didn't know.

"You followed me?" she finally settled with as his face came into focus. Scruff grew on his cheeks and chin. His eyes looked blue and intense. Blood covered his shoulder.

Her blood?

"I was trying to make sure you stayed out of trouble," Mark said.

Her heart raced. Had he seen everything? That would mean he was a witness also. That it wouldn't just be her word against Sol's. "You saw the drop?"

"I did." He glanced toward the scene of the accident, toward the driver who'd T-boned her.

That's when it hit her. The other driver had stared at her after she'd been hit. He was alive.

And she hadn't run a red light.

She'd been hit on purpose.

Just then, the man leaped from his truck and began running down the road.

"Go!" Laney raised her arm and pointed.

Mark hesitated only a moment before darting after the man.

Laney watched as they disappeared around the corner. Just as they did, the paramedics arrived.

"We need to take you to the hospital," a paramedic said.

"I'll be fine," she insisted. She was surprisingly unscathed. But how much more could her body endure? Would the next incident be the one that finished her off for good?

And why had Mark really been following her?

"Ma'am, I really think it's a good idea that you get checked out."

"No, really, I'm okay." No more hospitals. She needed freedom. It felt like this whole situation was a ticking time bomb.

She only hoped that Mark caught the man who'd hit her.

Mark pushed himself as hard as his body would allow as his feet pounded against the pavement. The man had too much of a head start. The distance between them seemed insurmountable.

Mark dodged pedestrians, skirted around a crowd gathered at a bus stop and pushed by a man selling rugs on the busy street. He couldn't lose sight of the other driver. The answers were so close. All the man had to do was trip up once, and Mark would catch him. He could settle this once and for all.

An intersection loomed in the distance. Tension grew between Mark's shoulders. This could be the moment where everything fell apart or came together.

A surge of speed shot through him as the urgency of the matter pressed on him harder.

Just then the man darted out in traffic.

Horns honked. Cars swerved. Brakes screeched.

The man pressed himself into the hood of an Impala that came dangerously close to running him over. He glanced back at Mark, and his eyes widened.

Then he darted away, even faster than before.

Mark soaked him in, trying to remember as many details as possible. The man had dark hair with a touch of wave. He was tall, thin and fit. He wore black, including a leather coat with the collar turned up.

Cars stopped at the intersection formed a blockade in front of them. Mark tried to dart around them, but they were bumper-to-bumper.

As he looked up, he spotted a car pull up to the curb. The man he'd been chasing jumped into the backseat. Just as Mark reached them, they squealed away. He glanced at the license plate, but it was gone.

Mark stopped in his tracks, knowing it was too late to catch them. His hands went to his hips as frustration took over. He'd been close. So close.

Using his cell, he put out an all-points bulletin for the car. Maybe another officer would catch it before the man got away.

All of this only confirmed what he already knew: whoever had rammed Laney had done it on purpose.

He started back toward where he'd left her, praying that she was okay. Praying that she would live to see another day. As he walked down the sidewalk, his phone rang. It was Jim. "We lost her."

"What?" Alarm rushed through him. Laney? Had something happened to Laney?

"Traffic was heavy and she took us on a crazy chase through town. It sounds staged, but a train actually cut us off."

"You're talking about the brunette," Mark muttered, relief flushing his heart. All he'd been able to think about was Laney sustaining injuries from the accident that hadn't taken effect until later. The concern he felt was surprising. He always cared about the people involved in his cases, but his concern this time felt staggering.

The thought threw him off guard. He couldn't give in to his emotions. That only ended in disaster every time.

But there was something about Laney that seemed different. In the short time he'd known her, she'd surprised him. She was intelligent and kind. Smart and trusting. Scared but strong.

Those were combinations he didn't always see. Even when he wasn't with her, his thoughts drifted toward her and they went beyond the investigation. He pictured what it might be like to come home to someone like her. To actually feel hope for the future. To feel a sense of real community in his life, one that went beyond the police department.

He'd long since buried his dreams of happily growing old. His family had been stripped away from him. The one woman he thought he'd loved had only used him. All of it was enough to make him want to seclude himself.

Maybe he didn't follow through on that like Laney did. He didn't have a job where he could work at home alone without ever having to interact with people. But, in another way, they were very much the same.

The past had altered their futures—and not for the better.

Maybe he needed to change that. But he was going to have to do a lot of praying to get himself to that place emotionally.

"Of course I'm talking about the brunette," Jim said. "Who did you think I was talking about?"

"Never mind. Did you run the plates?"

"We did. The car was stolen from a place out in Mechanicsville yesterday. We got nothing on the driver."

Of course. Mark wasn't even surprised. Whoever was doing this was good. They'd covered all of their tracks and made certain not to make mistakes.

"How about the business, CybCorp. Anything on that yet?"

"Nah, Williams is on his way up there to check it out."

"Thanks, Jim."

"Yeah, I'll keep you updated."

When he reached Laney, he found her arguing with paramedics.

"I've got this," he told them.

They stared at him a moment and finally shrugged, probably happy to hand her off to someone else. It was time to get her somewhere safe—whether she liked it or not.

"So this is your friend's house?" Laney asked, staring at the brick ranch house set back on a couple acres of property. It was charming with neat shrubs in the flowerbeds, and a porch swing welcoming guests near the front door.

A home. She'd had one of those at one time. She'd just spent the past hour on the drive here talking to the insurance company. It was going to be a long process before anything would be restored. Those were things she needed to think about later, though. She had other more pressing concerns at the moment.

Small cuts scratched her face, but the medics had put ointment on them. She also had a bump on her forehead, but Mark had been given strict instructions on what to watch for in case of a concussion.

She wasn't going back to the hospital, though. She was going to be fine.

They climbed out and walked toward the house.

"That's right," Mark said, unlocking the door. "They should be back later on this evening. I already talked to them and they're fine with you staying here. Trent's a former cop, so he's a good one to be around. And his wife, Tessa, is a real sweetheart."

Mark locked the door behind them and extended his hand toward the living room at their left. Hesitantly, feeling out of her element, she followed him into the room. He lowered himself onto a chair, but his muscles still looked alert.

"Why don't you sit for a minute?" Mark said.

She knew once she stopped moving that she'd be finished for a while. Her body was pleading with her to slow down and rest, but her mind raced full-speed ahead.

Laney rubbed her hands on her jeans and nodded, finally conceding to being seated. "I can't believe that lady got away," she murmured, replaying the scene over and over, and asking herself what she could have done differently.

"What were you doing at Sol's place of employment? And on the weekend, at that?" Mark leveled his gaze with her, getting right to the point.

She ignored the queasy feeling in her gut. She knew he'd followed her, but the thought still unnerved her. "I just wanted to talk to him. He works weekends a lot."

"What did you want to talk to him about?"

She let out a heavy sigh, the familiar feeling of having the weight of the world on her shoulders returning again. "I don't know. And that's the truth. I just want answers, and I wondered if Sol knew more than he's letting on."

"You're probably not the person to get those answers."

Ouch. But he'd spoken the truth. "I realize that. But I'm desperate."

"Don't do something stupid in that desperation."

His words hit her somehow. She pinched the skin between her eyes. She couldn't deny what he'd said. She was acting recklessly. But everything was on the line—everything. Not just her life, but Sarah's also. She couldn't just sit back and do nothing.

"It looks like the fire in your house was started by an electrical problem, by the way," Mark said quietly. "I talked to the fire marshal a few minutes ago."

Her sorrow only deepened at his words. Her house. All of her memories of her time with Nate. It was all gone now. "I'm sure that's what it was. An accident or a coincidence."

"They're not done investigating yet, Laney."

Suddenly, everything hit her. Maybe it was the car crash just now. Or the near catastrophe at the frozen yogurt shop earlier. Or the way she'd been drugged. Or accused of kidnapping. She supposed she could take her pick of any of those.

But the future seemed daunting at the moment, so much so that tears sprang to her eyes. She hung her head, wishing Mark wasn't here to see all of this. The tears had been bound to come eventually, though.

"I'm sorry, Laney." Mark's words sounded so kind and compassionate that they only made more moisture rush to the surface.

"No, I'm sorry."

"You've been through a lot over the past twenty-four hours. Anyone would break under the pressure. All things considered, I think you're doing pretty well."

She grabbed a tissue from the end table and dabbed under her eyes. "It's just that everything about my past was in that house. My parents are deceased, and I had my mom's old jewelry. My dad's flag for his military service. Then there was Nate and all of the reminders of our life together…"

His frown deepened. "You said it's been three years?"

"Sometimes it feels like decades and other times like weeks."

"The good news is that we always carry parts of our past in our heart. You can't ever lose that."

His words brought a strange comfort to her, but also the realization that he spoke from experience. "Thank you. It sounds like you know a thing or two about that."

He cleared his throat. "You could say that. I lost my sister eight years ago."

Compassion panged through her. "I'm so sorry."

"Me too. She was a great girl."

"If you don't mind me asking, what happened?"

A shadow passed his gaze. Laney wanted to take the question back, but didn't want to at the same time. Her death had obviously been a pivotal time in his life and Laney wanted to know more.

"My stepdad abducted her and killed her," he finally said.

Her hand went over her mouth. She couldn't even fathom what that would have been like. "I'm so sorry," she said again for lack of a better response.

He nodded, stoic and stiff. "When my stepdad found out he'd been discovered as the perpetrator in the crime, he shot my mom and then killed himself."

"You lost everything too…" She hadn't meant to say it aloud, but it was so unusual for her to meet people who could understand her pain. Most people her age hadn't experienced the loss she had. They had no idea what it felt like to have everything stripped away.

"That's so awful. I'm so sorry," she said once more.

"Thank you."

"Have you ever been married, Mark?" She wasn't sure where the question came from, but it slipped out. Maybe it was just curiosity. But she wondered if he had someone to go home to. If he had a wife who worried about him.

"No, I've never been married. Almost." He didn't offer any more information, and she didn't push it. She'd already asked far too many questions.

Just then, his phone rang. He put his cell to his ear, mumbled a few things, and then turned to Laney. "They just talked to Sol. Apparently he left a jump drive with information about his bank records and pin numbers on it. It was at the request of the kidnappers. They somehow managed to slip a note onto his car while he was at work."

Laney bit down for a minute. "Successfully avoiding being tracked by the FBI, who, I assume, are monitoring his phone calls."

"Of course. The police just brought Sol to the station to ask him some more questions. Maybe we'll know more soon. In the meantime, why don't you go get some rest?"

"That's probably a good idea," she said.

But she had no intention of resting. Not when so much was at stake.

ELEVEN

Laney waited until Mark lay back on the couch and closed his eyes. She could see that he was tired and knew it was just a matter of time before he fell asleep.

Soon enough, his breathing evened out and he was sleeping.

She grabbed the phone book, quickly looked up the number to a cab company and dialed. The man on the other line promised someone would be there within the next thirty minutes.

She glanced at Mark one last time, gratefulness filling her. God had been watching out for her when He sent Mark to investigate. She couldn't have asked for someone more kind or concerned. She hated to think about leaving him now, but she knew it was for the best.

Quietly, she tiptoed toward the door. She slowly turned the handle and the door creaked open. With one last look at the house, she slipped outside. Careful to remain on the edge of the driveway, she ran toward the road. That's where she'd instructed the cabdriver to pick her up.

Her pulse raced as she waited.

She hoped she didn't regret this. Though she felt like she could trust Mark, she couldn't tell him everything. Besides, doing so might put his career on the line. She couldn't do that.

Finally, a yellow cab appeared in the distance. She climbed in and shut the door, her heart slowing for a moment.

She'd done it. She'd managed to leave the house without alerting Mark. The task had felt impossible, and she'd half expected him to show up at any minute.

She mumbled an address to the driver. She didn't have much time. Not much time at all.

Any of the strides in friendship she'd taken with Mark would probably be gone after she did this. But what other choice did she have? This was no time to be a wallflower. Now was the time to be brave.

Besides, why should she feel a sense of loyalty to the man? Sure, he'd saved her life. He'd offered her a place to stay. He'd even shared details about his heartaches.

Had all of that created a false illusion that they were something more than a cop and a victim? That was crazy. She'd be wise to remember that. Mark would arrest her in a split second if he felt it necessary.

Her mind drifted back to their earlier conversation. His stepdad had killed his sister and then his mom before killing himself. What a horrific event to live through. She could only imagine how it had changed him. You didn't come through something like that unscathed.

Just like she hadn't gotten past Nate's death unaffected. She'd gone from happy-go-lucky to carrying the weight of their world on her shoulders. That's why the job with the CIA had been so perfect for her—it required her to do just that.

Nate, I miss you still. There will never be any one else like you.

As soon as the thought drifted from her mind, Mark's face appeared.

She shook her head. Mark wasn't Nate. There was no possibility of a future together with him. She'd be wise to keep reminding herself of that, even if she did start sounding like a broken record.

"Stop here," she told her driver. He pulled up to a curb beside the woods. She pulled out an extra twenty-dollar bill. "I need you to wait for me. I won't be long."

He shrugged. "Sure thing. But I'm only waiting for thirty. After that, I'm gone."

"Thank you." She slammed the door and pulled her coat tighter as she trudged through the woods.

She shouldn't do this. But she had no other choice.

When she pictured the disappointment in

Mark's eyes when he discovered what she'd done, it was almost enough to make her change her mind. Almost.

Finally, the woods cleared and she stepped through a gate and into a backyard. In the distance, she spotted the charred remains of her house. Grief gripped her heart for a moment.

She'd lost so much. She had to stop this before she lost any more.

Drawing in a deep breath of courage, she stepped toward another house, one that was still intact.

Anticipation tightened her muscles with each step.

Mark had said Sol was down at the police station. She had some time—but not a lot.

She rushed toward the back deck and moved a rock out of the way. A key rested beneath it.

Laney had joked with Sarah once that she could pretend to be locked out of her house and stay over at Laney's longer. But Sarah had told Laney that there was a backup house key and where it was kept.

Of course, Sol had a contingency plan. That was Sol for you. He always had a plan.

She grabbed the key and slid it into the lock. She'd had the taxi driver go past his house first to make sure there were no cars out front. When she hadn't seen any, she'd felt confident no one was home.

The lock clicked, and Laney slid the key back

in place before stepping inside. She'd been in there many times before.

The place was decorated minimally. The only things on Sol's walls were framed diplomas and pictures of antique maps and what appeared to be artifacts—nothing fancy. Nothing looked welcoming or warm.

Her gaze scanned the place now. Where did she start? What was she even looking for?

She wasn't sure. She only knew that she'd know when she found it.

Moving slowly, cautiously, she stepped through the living room. There was nothing unusual looking there. Everything appeared to be in place, from the TV remotes to every couch pillow. The place looked like a museum, like no one actually lived there.

She went into the office and opened the drawers. All she saw there were bills and envelopes and stamps. Nothing that grabbed her attention or seemed like it'd be helpful. If only any useful evidence could be marked as just that—it would make her job so much easier.

Her muscles continued to tighten the longer she was in the house. She was risking everything by being in there. Was it worth it?

She hoped so.

Upstairs or the basement? The basement, she decided. She'd never been down there before.

She pulled on the cord of a single light leading down the stairs. Chills raced up her spine. She'd never liked basements, especially dark ones. There were very few people she would do this for, but Sarah was one of them.

She hated to think that Sarah's own father might hold the answers in her disappearance, but that was exactly what Laney was beginning to think.

Why didn't she trust Sol? She asked herself as she traveled downward. Was it just a gut feeling? Was it because he'd never liked her? Because Sarah had started having problems with him?

It was hard to say.

At the bottom of the steps, the overhead light seemed to be even dimmer and more out of touch with the rest of the room. Another shiver raced through her. She pulled up the flashlight on her phone and shone it on the floor.

Bingo.

This was the place where Sol put everything he wanted out of sight. There were boxes and boxes of items down here, each organized to the max and complete with labels. Where did she even begin?

She looked at the words on each one. Some had years written there. Others had labels like "Mom and Dad's." She pulled down one with photos.

Inside, there were pictures of Sarah as a child. The girl was smiling and appeared happy. Her mother wasn't in any of these photos, Laney realized. What had Sarah told her? That her mom died in childbirth. That was right.

She flipped through several more pictures, both curious about Sarah's past and looking for clues. She couldn't help but think there was something missing. There was an album for nearly every year of Sarah's life in here.

Yet there were no photos of her as a baby. Had it been too painful for Sol to keep photos from that time in his life? Did the pictures remind him not only of what he'd gained during those years but what he'd lost?

Maybe Laney had been too hard on him. Maybe he was just as human and hurting as everyone else.

She put the photos back before carefully placing the box on the shelf. She sighed and ran a hand through her hair as she stared at the rest of the boxes. She'd never have time to go through all of these.

Lord, what am I doing? Am I totally out of line? Should I be praying for forgiveness right now?

She'd been stupid to come here, she realized. What kind of evidence did she hope to find? And in such a short amount of time, at that. It would take a team of detectives weeks to go through a house like this.

As she started back toward the stairs, ready to get back before Mark woke up, her flashlight caught something against the wall. What was that?

She paused. By all appearances, it was just a piece of insulation that had recently been replaced or moved. No big deal.

Despite that, she moved it.

Behind the insulation, against the wall, was an envelope. She slowly picked it up and undid the latch. Whatever was inside wasn't heavy or thick. Maybe a card of some sort?

Gingerly, she let the items slide out.

In her hand was a driver's license. A woman smiled in the corner. She was blonde, but besides the hair color, she bore a striking resemblance to Laney.

It was the woman from earlier today, Laney realized. What was Sol doing with her driver's license?

Her unease grew.

Before she could decide what to do with the license, she heard a footfall and then a deep voice said, "What do you think you're doing?"

Mark glared down at Laney. She'd thought she was being clever by sneaking out, but he'd heard her from the moment she opened the back door. He'd sprung from the couch and followed her. He'd even seen her grab the key from under the rock by Sol's back door and sneak inside.

He stomped down the stairs, wondering how he could have ever trusted her.

"Mark?" Laney's voice cracked as she said the word.

"Would you care to explain yourself before I arrest you for breaking and entering?"

Her eyes widened as he got closer. "It's not like that. You'll never believe what I just—"

"If this isn't breaking and entering, then what is?"

She frowned. "Mark, please."

"Maybe you should call me Detective James." His voice sounded steely, even to his own ears. But he'd obviously let himself become too comfortable around the woman. That had been a mistake. It always was.

"I had a feeling something was going on, and I was right. Mark—Detective James, please—"

He cut her off and grabbed her arm, ready to arrest her. "I'm going to have to take you in, Laney. I can't condone this."

"Please, just give me one minute. One minute."

She looked desperate. Absolutely desperate. He'd given her far too much credit. Never in a million years had he guessed she would do something like that.

"One minute. Starting now." He glanced at his watch.

She burst to life, her voice more animated with every word. "These driver's licenses were hidden here behind the insulation. It's the woman from today—except there are four different licenses, each with four different names on them, as well as four different states. But it's the same photo in each."

Something about her revelation sparked his interest. But he remained on guard as he glanced at the items in her hands. She was correct. But why would Sol have those?

"How do I know you didn't plant those there?" He had to be cautious. Laney might look innocent and sweet, but she was smart—smart enough to have a role in this.

"Why would I do that?" Her voice lilted with indignation as she stared up at him, fire dancing in her eyes.

"To set up Sol and make him look guilty."

Her bottom lip dropped slightly. "I repeat, why would I do that?"

He locked gazes with her, leaning closer. "To take attention off yourself?"

She leaned away, not backing down. "I thought I'd rightfully taken the attention off myself by almost getting killed at someone else's hands more than once."

"I agree that things are sketchy. We're all working hard to figure out what's going on."

"You're turning a blind eye to the most obvious suspect—Sol."

"We've looked into him. He had an alibi. Everyone at work saw him there."

"Maybe he's working with someone."

"Tell me this—how did you find that envelope?" He nodded toward the items in her hands. "You just happened to look on the other side of the insulation?"

"I did. I saw that it looked like it had been disturbed. I didn't really think I'd see anything there—"

"How do I know you didn't plant it there yourself?" He wasn't sure why he was hung up on that thought, but he was. He wanted to trust Laney; he did. But he had to be careful.

"Why would I go through all of that trouble? There would be an easier way to plant evidence against Sol than this. I'm a computer expert. I could hack into his email. His accounts. Breaking into people's homes is not my specialty."

Before he could ask any more questions, a door closed upstairs. Great. Sol was home.

He put a hand over his lips, slid the envelope back between the wall and nudged Laney into the shadows. Before joining her, he quickly tugged the light off, leaving them in total darkness.

This wasn't the way he was supposed to do police work. Not at all. In fact, he could lose his job over all of this. But he didn't want to be caught in someone's home, either. Not if there was a way around it. And not if there was even an ounce of truth in what Laney had told him.

He felt her tense in front of him.

How were they going to get out of this one?

He checked his watch. It was getting dark. Maybe Sol would be going to bed soon and they could sneak out. Otherwise, Mark would have no choice but to own up to what had happened. That meant confessing that Laney had broken into his home and that he'd followed after her.

As angry as he was with Laney, he wasn't quite ready to throw her to the wolves yet. Part of him still wanted to hold on to hope that she was one of the good guys. After all, there had been attempts on her life. She could be a victim here.

Those driver's licenses were interesting, though. Why were they here at Sol's? If Laney really wasn't behind this, then what was Sol up to? What was his connection to the brunette?

Footsteps creaked overhead, followed by voices. No, just one voice.

Sol must be on the phone. Mark couldn't make out what he was saying. It sounded garbled.

Don't come to the basement, he silently pleaded. He didn't want a complicated situation made even more complicated.

Despite his prayers, the basement door opened. Mark pushed Laney farther into the shadows and braced himself for whatever was about to happen.

Someone stomped down the stairs. What Mark heard made his lungs freeze.

It was Sol, and he was speaking a different language. Mark tried to identify it, but he couldn't.

Not Spanish, not French, not even German. So what was it?

Sol went to the section of the wall where the licenses had been hidden. He pulled the insulation back, plucked out the envelope and then started back upstairs.

As soon as the door closed, Laney stepped away from him and they exchanged a glance. Neither had to say anything to realize the gravity of what had happened.

Sol knew that envelope was there. He needed those driver's licenses now, for some reason. And he was speaking fluently in a foreign language that neither of them recognized.

They couldn't risk moving right now. There was still so much that could go wrong. But maybe Laney was telling the truth. And, despite her irresponsible actions, maybe she was just trying to find answers.

They stood close enough that Mark could feel her heart pounding against him. For some reason, the realization made his breath catch. Something about the woman brought out his urge to be a protector. He hadn't felt that way…in a long time. He never thought he'd feel that way again.

"We can't stay down here forever," Laney whispered.

Instinctively, his grip on her tightened. "I know that."

"What are we going to do?"

She spoke as if they were a team. In a way, they were—if he could ever figure out what she was hiding. But he still had a responsibility as an officer of the law. "I could still march you down to the station and arrest you."

"Isn't it obvious that I'm being set up?" she whispered, hitting each syllable hard.

It was becoming more and more apparent that someone was targeting her. But he had to remain cautious here. "We've both been down here in this basement long enough that I look guilty now too. That's a problem."

Indignation flashed in her gaze. "I didn't ask you to come after me."

"I have a duty to keep an eye on you."

She narrowed her eyes. "I never asked you to."

"I realize that."

"Please, don't do me any favors."

Before they could continue with their argument, the door closed upstairs. They both froze. Was that Sol? Had he left or had someone else come in?

Both remained silent for a moment, listening and waiting.

There were no footsteps. No more doors closing.

Just then a car started outside.

It appeared Sol had left.

He grabbed Laney's hand. "Come on. Let's

get out of here before we miss our window of opportunity."

He halfway expected her to push him away, but she didn't. She gripped his hand like a lifeline instead.

Slowly, they climbed up the stairs. Mark paused at the top and looked around. When he didn't see anyone, he tugged Laney's hand, pulling her behind him as he made a beeline toward the back door. Quietly, they slipped outside.

He breathed a sigh of relief. They'd made it out. But they weren't in the clear yet. They still had to get off Sol's property before anyone found them here.

He didn't wait for Laney to give an opinion. They ran toward the back fence, careful to stay in the shadows. They slipped out the back gate, ran through the woods until they came to his car. It wasn't until they were inside, both panting and expelling frosty breaths, that either relaxed.

"That was close," Laney said, leaning her head back against the seat, her lungs rising and falling rapidly.

"You don't have to tell me that."

She turned her head to face him better. "Did you recognize the language?"

He shook his head. "No. How about you?"

"No. No idea. I didn't realize he could speak another language so fluently. I always heard he was from Detroit. And what about those driver's licenses? Why would he have those?"

"I have no idea, Laney. But I intend to find out. If it's the last thing I do."

TWELVE

Laney's thoughts continued to turn over all of the new developments they'd learned today as Mark drove her to Trent and Tessa's house. Both were quiet on the drive, and Laney wondered if Mark's thoughts mirrored her own. So much had happened in such a short amount of time.

Back at the house, his friends were still not home. Apparently Tessa worked at an art museum and they had a big show this weekend that was keeping her busy. Trent had been along to help her. That was just as well with Laney. She could use some quiet time.

As soon as they walked in, Mark's phone rang. He excused himself as he put the phone to his ear and disappeared into the hallway.

Laney dropped onto the sofa, wanting desperately to process everything she knew. But all the information was almost too much to swallow. What did everything mean? How did the pieces fit together? She curled into the corner, longing for comfy pj's and a cat. She'd always wanted a cat. As soon as this nightmare ended, she was going to get one.

When Mark walked back into the room, his expression was grim. Was he about to chew her out again for sneaking into Sol's house? She couldn't blame him. It had been a risky idea. Yet, if she hadn't, she would have never seen the licenses. She would have never heard Sol speaking in an unknown language. Those two things had to mean something.

"Do you want to tell me what's going on?" Mark sat across from her and they locked gazes.

Here we go again. How many times did they have to go through this? "I thought I already explained everything to you. I'm just trying to find some answers—"

"That's not what I'm talking about. You're not telling me the truth about your job, are you, Laney?"

Her stomach clenched. "Why would you say that?"

"One of my guys just went to the address where the company is meant to be. There is no office there, Laney."

"What? What are you talking about? That's crazy. Of course there is." Her mind began racing. Was he telling the truth? What was going on?

"Laney, the building is empty. It's like the company never existed."

"That's impossible." Or was it? She'd been told that people actually worked in the office there, even though the company itself was a cover. Had she been mistaken?

Details flooded back to her. She'd only spoken with one person at the company, and she only had one phone number. All of her other interactions had been via the web. Nicholas was her only contact there, and he'd never had her up to the office for any special training or workshops.

"Laney, what are you thinking?"

She stood and began pacing, trying to make peace with her thoughts. She had to be off track here. The conclusions she was drawing...they were crazy. Out there. There was no way any of that was true.

"Laney?"

Mark's voice sounded right behind her. She turned and nearly collided with him. He caught her arms and stared her down.

"Talk to me," he urged.

That's when she realized her hands were trembling. She could hardly breathe. And this had nothing to do with her auto accident or any of the other attempts on her life.

She was beginning to see the bigger picture here, and it chilled her to the bone.

"I need a computer," she whispered.

Before she could look for one here at the house,

Mark held her tighter. "Laney, I need you to talk to me."

Her gaze flickered up toward his. His blue eyes looked steady. They begged for her trust. Pleaded for the truth.

Could she trust him? Could she tell him everything? At best, he might feel sorry for her. At worst, he'd think she was an idiot.

But they might not ever find the answers unless she shared her realization.

"I work for the CIA," she muttered, her mouth feeling like sawdust as the words left her lips.

His eyebrows shot up in surprise. "What?"

She nodded halfheartedly. "I was recruited three years ago to help them test various protocols for breaking through firewalls. Basically, we ran through scenarios together—what would happen if China tried to hack into the US treasury? Or how would we handle it if the personal information on our country's leaders was leaked? We just finished a big project where we set up programs and safeguards."

They both sat down on the couch and faced each other. It was a good thing because her knees had started to shake.

"Tell me more," he urged.

"A man named Nicholas recruited me. He'd been following my work with Blueleaf software and said he thought I was one of the best. He offered me a chance to serve my country, to work from home. You have to understand that I didn't want to leave my home for the longest time after Nate…"

"I understand."

"This job gave me the opportunity to do that. I said yes and began working for them. Nicholas was my contact."

"Did you ever go to the CIA headquarters?"

She shook her head. "No, I didn't. I was told that I was a contractor for them, but that my job was classified. That's why they set up a cover organization that I worked for. They gave me a special computer. Every week they sent me my job schedule, and we mostly communicated via email."

"Do you have that computer?"

"No, you do. Or the police department does. I went back to get it."

"I see." He sounded skeptical.

As he should be. Now that she was voicing the story aloud, she realized it sounded outlandish. Because her job was classified, she'd never said any of this out loud before.

"Did you ever meet Nicholas face-to-face? Maybe when they gave you the computer for your job?"

"No, I never did. Everything was done by delivery or email. I didn't think anything of it…"

"But?"

She forced herself to meet his gaze. "I'm beginning to realize that I was duped."

A knot formed between his eyes. "What do you mean?"

"I mean—what if none of that was real? Even worse—what if the people who hired me weren't the CIA at all? What if they were the opposite? If they're people who hate the US, and I'm helping them bring down the government I thought I was working for and ruin our country?"

Mark tried to process everything Laney had just told him. The CIA? He would have never in a million years guessed the conversation would go there. But now some of the vague answers she'd given him about her job made sense. That's what she'd been hiding.

He leaned over her, watching as she tapped at Trent's computer. She'd managed to find her way onto the server she'd used in her previous position with the CIA—or whatever company it really was—and she was attempting to disable it. He couldn't begin to understand everything she was typing and doing at the moment, but she almost looked frantic.

"Explain to me again what this might do in the wrong hands?"

She continued to face the computer, not slowing a bit as she talked. "It would open up a wormhole into US accounts. The US Treasury. The stock markets. The Department of Defense. Homeland Security. Think of the most secure computer systems possible. This program I created could give the wrong person access to that information and what they could do with it…it could be deadly, devastating."

Tension grew between his shoulders. It sounded like the invention of the atom bomb—only for the computer. It had the potential to be catastrophic. "Are you sure you can disable it?"

"I'm doing my best. I created it. I only fear these guys have already begun using it for the wrong reasons."

His mind continued to race, trying to think through each detail. "If you're able to do this, they'll know that you're on to them, right?"

She grimaced but continued to type. "Possibly. But it's a risk I have to take."

Mark straightened and rubbed his eyes a moment. Did this somehow tie in with Sarah? How? Why would these terrorists kidnap Laney's neighbor's daughter?

Unless… Sol was a part of this somehow. He had the driver's license of one of the supposed kidnappers. He spoke a different language.

Still, why would he kidnap his own daughter?

Mark was going to have to call his captain soon and fill him in on everything he'd learned. The situation would have to be handled delicately, though.

"There." Laney leaned back, her fingers leaving the keyboard for the first time in an hour. "I did it. The program is disabled. I think I was able to reroute my location. Under ordinary circumstances, they'd be able to trace where the server breach came from, but I made the signal ping from different locations, so we should be safe. For now."

He pressed his lips together before asking, "Laney, do you think Sol could be involved in this?"

"I think it's a strong possibility." She shifted. "Is there a way to look into his background, Mark? To see if he has any ties with foreign nationals or terrorists?"

"I can probably arrange that. But we'll have to be very discreet."

Laney was able to borrow some clothes from Tessa. She forced herself to take a long, hot shower and change into fresh jeans and a flannel T-shirt.

Earlier she'd met the gracious couple who'd opened up their home. Both had seemed affable and concerned. The two had just gotten married a couple of months ago and seemed over-the-moon happy together.

As Laney dried her hair, she thought once more about how everything was starting to catch up with her—the accident, the overdose, the upheaval of her life. It was playing on her both mentally and physically. She even looked tired, she realized as she stared in the foggy mirror. She didn't want to take any pain medication, but she did it anyway. She wouldn't be worth anything tomorrow if she didn't get some rest.

After she felt more presentable, she went downstairs, following the aroma of something savory. When she walked into the dining room, everyone was seated, eating lasagna, bread and a salad.

Mark stood, his eyes widening for a moment— widening enough that she felt her face grow hot.

It's not because he's attracted to you, she rationalized. *He's just being polite.*

"Excuse us one minute," he mumbled. He pulled Laney into the other room and plopped something into her hands. "This is your new phone. It's untraceable."

"What...? When...? Why?"

"It's in case these kidnappers try to contact you. We switched your old number onto this one and transferred all your contacts. Someone from the department dropped it off for me while you were in the shower. I wanted to give it to you immediately."

She slid it into her pocket. "Thank you."

She already felt better. At least she had a means of communicating now if she needed it—and the likelihood that she would need it was high.

Together they walked back toward the table.

"You did join us!" Tessa stood. "I'm so glad."

The woman was thin with blond curly hair to her shoulders. She had an easy smile, and beamed every time she looked at her husband. Laney already liked her, and they'd just met less than two hours ago.

Her husband, on the other hand, was tall and broad with a square jaw and an intense gaze. He had close-cropped, curly blond hair with a tint of red. When he'd first introduced himself, he'd joked with her, apologizing that she had to be paired with Mark. His lighthearted banter had made him seem approachable.

"I'm not sure how long I'll last," Laney muttered. "I took some extra-strength pain reliever, and it's probably going to knock me out."

"Understood. Nothing like sleeping with a full stomach, though."

Mark pulled out a chair for her. She muttered thanks, thinking about the last time someone had done that for her.

It had been Nate. She hadn't dated since then. She'd hardly been social. By most people's standards, she *hadn't* been social.

Her stomach fluttered. Mark was just being polite. There was nothing else behind the action. But for some reason it still made her feel special.

"So we hear you're a computer genius," Trent said.

Laney exchanged a glance with Mark. He was

careful. She knew he had been. And she too had
to be cautious with how much information she
shared. "I know a thing or two about how to get
around online."

"We saw the news story on TV about the missing girl," Tessa said. "I'm sorry to hear that. I understand you two were close."

She nodded, laying a napkin in her lap. "It's
true. She's a special girl. I just pray she's okay."

"We'll pray with you."

Thankfully, the rest of the dinner conversation turned from Laney to general chitchat. Apparently, Mark and Trent went way back. They'd
gone to the police academy together. They had
another friend named Zach Davis who'd been a
part of their trio, and apparently Zach had recently gotten engaged himself.

Laney's mind drifted from the conversation
as she fought to remain lucid. Had she done everything to shut down that program she created?
She knew she had.

But how could she have been so naive? How
could she have really thought she'd been working for the CIA? She'd always been smart. She'd
gotten straight As and a perfect GPA. But when
Nicholas had called her, she'd been reeling for the
loss of Nate. She'd been secluded and had lost her
sense of purpose. That job offer had been like a
lifeline to her.

Just then, her cell phone rang.

Panic raced through her.

She glanced at the screen.

It was Nicholas! She showed his name to Mark, realizing her hands were trembling so badly that it would be hard for him to read the screen. "What should I do?"

His hand covered hers until her limb stopped shaking. As he read the screen, his jaw clenched. "You should answer."

Drawing in a deep breath, she put the phone to her ear and stepped out of the room. Mark followed her, staying close and leaning in to hear better.

"Hello?" Her voice trembled slightly as she answered.

"Laney? Where have you been? I've been emailing you."

She decided to play along, to act like she didn't know what was going on. Nicholas wasn't stupid, though. He was playing some kind of game right now also.

"I haven't been able to access my emails," she finally said.

"Then how were you able to work on the program? I just got on, and it appears you changed something."

She closed her eyes, praying that she'd handle this correctly. "I was just working on a few things. Trying to keep my mind occupied. A lot has happened. I've been trying to call you. You haven't answered."

"Haven't answered? You know I'm always there for you. You must have dialed the wrong number."

She fought the outrage that welled in her. He must think she was an idiot. She had no doubt she'd dialed the right number.

She took a deep breath before saying, "I didn't. I also know that the front organization you set up to cover who I was really working for is gone. You told me there was a physical office space in case someone got suspicious. What's going on? I feel like you've hung me out to dry."

"Don't be silly. Can't you see we're being set up? Someone discovered what we're doing and they're trying to wreak havoc for us."

"Who do you work for, Nicolas?" Anger burned in her as she asked the question. She may have been fooled once, but it wouldn't happen again.

"I told you. The US government."

"Stop lying to me. Who do you really work for?" Her brain felt fuzzy, possibly from the high dosage of pain medication she'd taken. But she couldn't let that stop her. "Besides, listen to yourself. At first you said I should have been able to reach you and then you acknowledged that the cover we set up for this job is gone. Which is it?"

He didn't say anything for a moment. "Laney, what kind of lies are those people feeding you?"

She tensed and glanced at Mark. "Those people? What are you talking about?"

Something suddenly didn't feel right. How had he known she was with other people? Working with other people?

"Laney, you need to let me through that firewall." His voice turned from friendly and concerned to a low, menacing growl.

She raised her chin, more determined than ever. "No. Not until you tell me who you're working for."

"Laney, this isn't your property. We hired you to do a job."

Mark gave her a nod of affirmation, the action giving her just enough courage to continue. "I thought I was working for my country. That's not the case."

"This is your last warning, Laney." His voice went beyond a growl now. It was downright threatening.

"Or what?" Just as she said the words, the front window broke.

Shots filled the night air.

THIRTEEN

Mark threw Laney on the ground before grabbing his gun. "Get behind the couch. Now!"

Laney didn't argue. She scrambled across the floor until the couch separated her from the string of gunfire that had erupted. His heart pounded into his ears as shots continued to ring out.

Trent? Tessa? Were they okay?

As if to answer his question, he heard Trent yell from the other room. He turned his head in time to see Trent pull out his gun and rush for cover near the window at the back of the house.

Tessa hid beneath the table, her eyes wide with fear—but also with strength. She'd been on the run for her life before and knew how to handle herself.

More gunfire sounded from outside.

How many men were out there? Mark didn't even have a good guess. Right now, he had to focus on keeping everyone alive.

He darted to the couch, careful to keep Laney covered, he raised his gun and fired back.

As he did, another bullet hit the glass picture above the table, shattering it into hundreds of pieces. Laney gasped beneath him as shards of crystal rained down.

This was a full-on attack. Men had located them, surrounded the house, and they were determined to massacre everyone inside. Mark couldn't let that happen.

"Call for backup!" he shouted.

Aiming carefully, Mark caught sight of a man outside one of the windows. He fired, and the man moaned before falling to the ground.

One down. But how many more were outside the house?

As another string of bullets littered the inside of the house, concern ricocheted through him.

He didn't want this to end badly. But they'd been ambushed. The men outside had trapped them in the house.

"Do you have another gun?" Laney whispered. "Let me have it."

He wasn't in a position to argue. He reached for his ankle holster and pulled out his backup weapon.

"You know what you're doing?" he whispered.

"Kind of."

That wasn't entirely comforting, but he didn't have time to argue. He only knew if these men got ahold of Laney, it was more than her future at stake.

A bullet skimmed dangerously close to his head.

"Mark, watch out!" Trent yelled.

He ducked to the ground just as another bullet headed his way. It crashed into the table leg behind him.

Trent fired back, hitting another one of the men outside the house.

Mark rolled onto his side and let out a line of gunfire.

At the moment, sirens sounded outside Trent's house. The noise must have spooked the remaining men because the gunfire went silent.

They weren't getting away that easily, though.

Mark hopped up from the floor and took off after them. His legs burned as he rushed through the house. As soon as he stepped outside, he saw the men jump into a van before it squealed away.

Again.

The men had gotten away again.

They were always one step ahead of them.

As he stood there in the front yard, three police cars and an ambulance pulled up. Jim jumped out. "Everything okay?"

He explained what had happened. Two police cars took off down the road, but knowing these guys, they were already long gone.

Mark walked back inside and found the rest

of the crew. Tears were running down Laney's cheeks and Tessa was attempting to comfort her. The house looked like it was in a war zone, and Mark felt a pang of regret. He shouldn't have come here. His two friends had just started their lives together, and now everything was destroyed.

He saw Tessa scoot away as he approached Laney. He put a hand on her arm, surprised by the jolt of electricity he felt at their touch. There was definitely something there between them— something that had developed quickly. But this wasn't the time or place to explore it.

"This is all my fault," she whispered.

"No, it's not." Against his better judgment, he pulled her into a hug. It was against his professional standards, but the woman needed someone. He couldn't just let her stand there looking alone and without a person in the world who cared.

"I shouldn't have come here. I almost got your friends killed."

"I was the one who brought you here, so blame me. Besides, Trent isn't someone to be messed with. He can hold his own."

"How about the two guys who were shot?"

"They got away. The van who'd taken the other guys probably picked them up. They left a trail of blood, but they were obviously still alive. Who knows for how long."

She shook her head and dabbed her eyes again. "Nicholas and his men must have been following me this whole time. That's the only way to explain how they know where I've been. They knew I was in the hotel. They knew I was driving down the road when they T-boned me."

"Stop being so hard on yourself." His voice was firm and unwavering as he nudged her, desperate to pull her from the dark pit of her self-reprimand.

"How can I not be? This is a matter of national security, and I keep messing up. I've ruined so many people's lives. And this isn't even done yet."

He leaned down until her gaze connected with his. He had to get through to her using whatever means necessary. "There's something I realized, Laney. Now that you've changed the firewall to this program, these men probably won't try to kill you. They need you."

She pulled her head up. "So they'll just try to abduct me?"

"It's a possibility. That whole attack back there—I think they wanted to bring you in alive. You're no good to them dead."

A small gasp escaped and her voice sounded desperate. "But they were shooting at us. At me."

"They had good aim. They could have taken you down at the beginning if they wanted to. When I examined the direction where the bullets came from, I realized you were the only one out of the three of us that these guys had in clear line of site through the windows. But they kept you alive. It was the rest of us they wanted dead."

Her lips quivered. "What am I going to do?"

"We'll figure it out. Jim is looking into the driver's licenses now."

Her wide eyes filled with gratitude first, then concern. "You said 'we'? You should get away now while you can."

He straightened, remembering his role in all of this. His many conversations with his captain wafted through his thoughts. His captain expected him to find answers. He expected Laney to lead them to the truth.

"I'm afraid I'm a part of this, whether I like it or not," he finally said.

Her eyes almost reminded him of a child's as she stared up at him. "Because you tried to help me?"

His jaw flexed, the reality of the situation settled in with a vengeance. "Because I'm doing my job."

She nodded and stepped back, as if his words were a reminder to her that there were boundaries in place. And there *were*—he'd be wise to remember that.

He rolled his shoulders. "Listen, I need to call my captain. Then we need to get you out of here. Because if those guys manage to capture you, you're right—the security of our country is on the line."

Several hours later, Laney was back in Mark's car. Both the FBI and Homeland Security had questioned her mercilessly. The agencies would be involved in this case from here on out and they'd made it clear just how dire this situation was. The FBI would be searching for Sarah, and Sol would be questioned again.

Trent and Tessa had been temporarily rehoused until the threat passed. Laney had apologized to them profusely, and they'd been both kind and understanding.

Laney had no idea where Mark was taking her, and she didn't even bother to ask. Though her medication had made her feel sluggish at first, the situation at the house had kick-started her adrenaline and now she felt wide-awake, which was too bad. Sleep seemed like an escape, something she wished was an option right now.

It wasn't.

It had been one thing when she was in danger. But now she was starting to realize just how many other people were in jeopardy because of her. Because she'd been naive, now Mark was in peril. Trent and Tessa. Sarah.

And most of all, her country was vulnerable for attack. Her ability to trust too easily, as well as her naivete, had placed national security at risk. What had she been thinking?

"Hey," Mark said softly.

She glanced away from the window and toward him but said nothing. The darkness outside, in one way, was comforting. It masked things she couldn't see. But, in another way, it reminded her of the uncertainties of the future.

"What are you thinking about?" Mark said.

She rubbed her lips together before answering more honestly than she'd expected. "The fact that I don't know how to fix this."

He squeezed her arm. "We'll find answers, Laney."

She shook her head, unable to play the role of the helpless victim anymore. She'd gotten herself into this mess, she had to get herself out of it. "You keep saying 'we.' But this is my problem, Mark."

"This is everyone's problem, Laney. We have a whole team of men working on it. I know I said this earlier, but don't be so hard on yourself. These men are clever. They knew exactly what they were doing, and they've been planning this for a long time. They were the ones who pulled you into this."

"I do need to be hard on myself. I should have been more careful. I should have asked for more confirmation when I was offered that job. But everything these guys sent me seemed so official. They even *sounded* official. And, because the CIA is covert and secretive, I didn't think twice about how vague they were. I really thought they were the real thing."

"The best criminals are able to easily deceive people."

She shrugged. "I guess I also needed to feel like I was contributing to something again, that I needed some kind of connection to the world. To life, for that matter." She sighed. "I feel like a fool."

"You weren't." He squeezed her arm again. "We'll solve this. I promise you."

A grateful smile tried to curl her lips, but the action didn't succeed. "Thank you."

Mark glanced in the rearview mirror.

"Are we being followed?" Laney asked.

"No, I don't think so. I just want to be careful."

A few minutes later, Mark pulled to a stop in front of an old cabin about an hour outside of Richmond. The building looked warm and cozy as the light glowed in the windows of the two-story house. Miles and miles of woods appeared to surround it.

"This is going to be your home for a while," Mark said, as they sat in the gravel drive for a moment.

"Where are we?"

"A safe house. We'll have two officers stationed here, as well. We can't risk you being captured."

Laney nodded, wishing that so many things in her life weren't out of her control. She had to do something to take the reins again. She glanced at

Mark, silently pleading that he would understand. "Is there a computer here?"

"Probably. Why?"

"I need to do some research."

"We have people doing that for you."

She swung her head back and forth, leaving no room for doubt. "I can do it better."

A wrinkle formed between his eyes. "What do you mean?"

She shrugged self-consciously, knowing she had to open up about the not-so-pleasant things she'd done. "There may have been a time in my life when I learned a bit about hacking."

"What?"

She sighed, recalling a part of her past she wasn't proud of. "It's true. I told myself I needed to learn how to hack in order to be a better computer programmer. It was a short-lived hobby of mine. As soon as I met Nate, I realized I needed to stay far away from that kind of life."

A hint of amusement glinted in his eyes. "I can't condone something like that, Laney."

"I didn't ask you to. But I need answers. I don't have time to waste."

"Anything you learn…we wouldn't be able to use legally."

"I'm not concerned with the legal ramifications. I'm concerned with people's lives."

Finally he nodded. "I'm not making any promises, but I'll see what I can find."

A surge of excitement and fear shot through her. Maybe this was her chance to make things right. To *really* make things right.

She hoped with every fiber of her being that that was the case.

FOURTEEN

Laney posed her fingers over the keyboard, ready to do what she did best. She never thought her skills would come in handy in this way. But now she was glad she knew what she did.

She needed more information on Sol Novak. Somehow, he was a link here. She needed to find out why.

Her temporary home had three bedrooms. The computer was located in the downstairs bedroom, at a corner desk. The whole place was dark with dim lights and dark wooden walls. It smelled like cedar and the warm fireplace made the place seem welcoming, despite the armed officers standing guard at the doors.

She couldn't wait to research Sol Novak herself. She needed more information. More than one person depended on her getting some answers, and she knew she had the capabilities to locate what was needed faster than law enforcement.

"What website do you plan on hacking, exactly, to get this intel?" Mark asked, standing behind her.

She was all too aware of his presence. How could she not be? It was strong, imposing. He was that kind of person. And she hated herself for thinking that. Guilt pounded at her. What about Nate? The fact that she was even attracted to Mark made her feel like she was betraying her husband.

But Nate had been gone three years. She'd mourned his death. In some ways, she'd always mourn his death. He'd been her first love. She'd seen herself growing old with him. That wasn't something that could easily be forgotten.

She shoved those thoughts away as various screens blurred across the computer. She almost felt like she was on autopilot as she broke through firewall after firewall in order to find protected data.

"I started with a simple internet search, and I'm going from there." She typed in Sol's name, and pages of search results popped up. Most of the facts there were what she already knew. He worked at an accounting firm. He was forty-seven. He'd won a golf tournament once.

"Hmm." She leaned back, her mind racing.

"What?"

She stared at the screen, trying to balance the facts with her assumptions. "I find it interesting that there's no mention of Sol until twelve years ago."

Mark shrugged. "The internet wasn't really popular until recent years, so maybe that's not unusual."

"Maybe. That could be true. But usually there's *something*. An article. A mention. A social media hit." With that, she straightened, another notion hitting her like a lightning rod. "I have another idea."

"What's that?"

Her fingers flew across the keyboard, trying to keep up with her thoughts. "I want to find out about Sol's wife."

"What does she have to do with any of this?"

"Maybe nothing. Maybe something. It's anyone's guess at this point."

Mark leaned closer, still focused on the computer screen. "What happened to her?"

"Sarah told me she died during childbirth. I'm going to search through marriage records and birth records to see what I can find out." A few taps of her keys later and she frowned before letting out another grunt. "That's interesting. I don't see anything about Sol ever being married."

Mark shifted behind her. "I'm sure there are a lot of sources out there with that information. Maybe you just have to hit the right website or database."

She shook her head. "But it would be listed here. This database is comprehensive."

"Why's that?"

She cast an apologetic glance his way before answering. "It's the social security administration. They have everyone's stats."

"You hacked in to social security?" His voice rose in pitch.

She twirled in the chair to better face him. "You didn't hear that from me."

He turned and paced away. "I wish I hadn't."

"Don't you think that's strange? There should be a record of their marriage. There should be something."

Mark continued pacing and shook his head as his eyes seemed to calculate their next move. "Look into Sarah's history, then. Her mother's name should be listed on the birth certificate. Maybe that will provide you with something, and give us more insight on Sol Novak."

"Great idea." Her fingers began flying across the keyboard again. It was almost second nature to her to do this, and it ignited a buried passion in her. It made her feel like she was in college again, having contests with students to see who could hack the fastest. "Hmm. That's weird."

"What now?"

She hit a few more keys, trying to make sure she wasn't missing anything. "I can't find Sarah's birth certificate."

Mark paused beside her, the tantalizing scent

of something piney and woodsy drifting toward her. She had to stay focused here.

"That's impossible," he said. "She obviously has a birth certificate. Maybe Sarah's not her real name."

"No, her name is Sarah. I had to write some references once for her when she applied for a scholarship. It was her full name. I'm certain of it."

"She has to have some kind of record," Mark continued. "Otherwise she couldn't get into public school. She didn't appear out of thin air."

Laney shook her head, nibbling on her fingernails, a bad habit that Nate used to always call her out on. "I'm telling you, there's no record of her birth. However—Sol spoke a different language, and he spoke it fluently. I wonder if he's lived somewhere else?"

Mark began pacing again, obviously feeling stressed out. Laney wished she could urge him to sit down. Maybe rub his shoulders. Do something to make him feel better.

But she knew she couldn't. She'd be overstepping her bounds. Despite the connection she felt with him, their relationship was strictly professional.

She'd be wise to continue to remind herself of that.

"The fact is that I can't bring up anything that we saw. If there's a case against Sol, it can't include that information we found illegally at his house. It would be thrown out in court."

"So what do we do?"

He rubbed his chin and let out a long sigh. "We have to find other evidence—the legal way."

"How?"

He nodded resolutely. "First thing in the morning, I'm going to go talk to him."

She twirled around in the chair so she could face Mark, so he could see her eyes. "I want to go with you."

He shook his head, leaving no room for doubt. "You can't. For so many reasons. Most of all, we need for you to remain hidden. It's imperative on more than one level. Do you understand?" His gaze locked on hers.

After a moment of thought she nodded. "Yes, I understand."

This was one argument she wouldn't win. She could see it in his expression, and he had a point—if someone was to abduct her and was able to manipulate her to use her abilities, they'd all be in trouble.

Upstairs there was a small sitting area with a couch and a TV. After Laney had finished on the computer, she and Mark sat there. He'd fixed them both some coffee, which she desperately needed in order to stay awake after the exhausting night had begun to stretch into the early morning.

"Can I ask you something?" Mark turned toward her and took a sip of his coffee. Laney realized that they were sitting closer than she'd planned. Close enough that she could feel his body heat, smell his piney scent. Near enough that she could easily reach up and feel the scruff on his cheek.

Not that she would do that.

She cleared her throat, urging her thoughts to stay on track. "Of course you can ask me something. Anything."

"At your house after Sarah had been abducted, you noticed that one section of the fence was uneven. How?"

She shrugged. "I've always had an eye for detail."

"My guys checked it. The fence was only off by half an inch."

She shrugged again. "I know it sounds weird but, at times, I have a neurotic obsession with what I notice. For example, did you know that one of your eyebrows is higher than the other? Or that, on the first day we met, I knew right away by how your tie was knotted that you're left-handed. Devon—the other guard downstairs—he recently got divorced. I can still see the lines from his wedding ring."

Mark nodded as if impressed. "You do have amazing powers of observation."

"I've always had an eye for things that are out

of place," she reminisced. "It used to drive Nate crazy. There was one time he put new tile in our bathroom. Honestly, it looked great. I wasn't going to say anything. But he noticed me looking at one spot, and eventually coerced me into admitting that the tile there was crooked. I try to stop myself. I really do. I'm usually not successful, though."

"I suppose that quality helps you when working with technology?"

"It does. I have to look for weaknesses in certain code. This is just the way God wired me. I used to want to change it, but now I just try to use it for good."

"I can admire that." He paused for a moment and studied her face. "You still miss your husband, don't you?"

She glanced down at her coffee mug, absently rubbing the side. "I do. I always will. But I also know that part of my life is behind me. I can't bring Nate back. He wouldn't want me holding on too tightly to the past. One of his favorite mottoes was Seize the Day."

"It's a good mantra to live by, especially with all the uncertainties in life."

She nodded, feeling a desperate need to change the subject. "How about you? You said you once came close to being married?"

He leaned back slightly as if more comfortable talking about Laney than himself. "Before my sister was abducted, I was living a not-so-admirable life. I was making a lot of money with my job in sales. I used it to impress the ladies. After she died, I dove into anything I could to drown the pain. I took it to an all new level. One day, it was like a switch flipped in me and I realized I had to…seize the day, I suppose."

"I can't even imagine you being anything but purposeful."

He heaved in a breath. "You might be surprised. After I joined the police force, I did meet someone. Her name was Chrystal. She was broken down on the side of the road, and I stopped to help her. We had an instant attraction."

"What happened?"

"I was in the middle of a big trial—the biggest in my career, up to that point. It was a woman who'd killed two people as she drove under the influence of drugs. This woman denied it. She claimed one of the prescriptions she was taking had an adverse effect on her. It was a hard case with a lot of circumstantial evidence."

Laney waited, curious to know where his story was going.

"It turned out that Chrystal was an old friend of this woman who was on trial. She'd been going through my notes whenever I turned my back. She was trying to find something that would clear her friend. A mistake I made. Procedural errors."

"She was using you?"

He pressed his lips together. "Unfortunately."

"How did you realize it?"

"I caught her going through some of my notes one day at the office. She'd stopped by for a visit—she did that often—and when I stepped away for a minute, she got nosy. She denied it at first, but then I started looking into her background. I realized that she had gone to the same high school as the defendant, and that they'd graduated the same year. That's when I broke things off with her."

"I can't imagine…"

"It wasn't my best moment."

"You couldn't have known."

"No, but I put a case in jeopardy, and I never want to do that again."

Something about his words made her jolt. Was he talking about her, as well? Did he think that his relationship with her was compromising this investigation?

"That makes perfect sense," she finally managed to get out. "Work is the most important thing. I mean, not work. People are—"

"I understand, Laney." His words sounded so gentle that they helped calm her anxiety.

"I'm rambling, aren't I?" She offered a sheepish smile.

He grinned. "Just a little."

"Sorry."

His smile faded, and he leaned closer, lowered

his voice. "You know, when all of this is over, I'd like to get to know you outside of this investigation, Laney Ryan."

Did he mean it? Especially given what he'd just said about the other case that he'd put in jeopardy. All along she'd thought her attraction was one-sided.

They stared at each other a moment. She could see it in his eyes that he wanted to kiss her. The thought made her breath catch.

They both leaned toward each other. Laney's heart reached into her throat, pounded into her ears, raced with anticipation.

Just as suddenly as it started, Mark pulled back and jumped to his feet. "I'd better get to bed before I do something I shouldn't."

Laney stood, feeling entirely too self-conscious. "Right. Of course. Me too."

He studied her another moment before taking a step back. "Good night, Laney."

She swallowed hard. "Good night, Mark."

That had been close. Too close. Even more confusing was the fact that, for a moment, she'd wished Mark hadn't stopped.

She knew one thing for sure: At least for tonight, the nightmares would take a backseat to dreams about Mark.

FIFTEEN

First thing the next morning, after a good night's rest, Mark and Jim met with Sol at his home. According to Jim, no money had been withdrawn from Sol's account and, even though the kidnappers had promised Sarah would be returned after he dropped off the jump drive, Sol claimed he hadn't heard from them again. He'd been apologetic about taking matters into his own hands, but had claimed he was desperate.

"You're looking into me? I'm a suspect?" Sol's face reddened as he sat across from them at his kitchen table. The man looked like he hadn't gotten any sleep in months. His hair, usually thin and too long on top, didn't lay in place, his shirt was wrinkled and bags hung under his eyes.

"No one said you were a suspect." Mark was careful to keep his voice even. "We're just exploring every angle possible right now. We don't want to leave any stone unturned."

"We thought maybe something in your past

connected with this case," Jim said. "We have to examine everything. You want that, don't you? For us to do whatever it takes for Sarah to come back?"

Sol sighed and hung his head before pinching the skin between his eyes. He seemed to be processing what they'd said and contemplating his options. Finally, he looked up, but his eyes looked burdened. "The fact is that I adopted Sarah."

Mark blinked, surprised at his revelation. "That's not what we heard."

Sol rubbed his fingers together on the table, a new melancholy washing over him. "I told Sarah that her mother died in childbirth. I didn't want her to ask too many questions or to make her feel like she'd been abandoned. But I adopted her at two years old. She doesn't even remember life without me."

"So you were never married?" Mark asked.

Sol shook his head sadly. "I'm afraid no woman would ever have me. I'm a bit of a bear to live with sometimes. But that didn't mean that I didn't want to have children."

Mark examined Sol as he spoke. He didn't show any signs of depression—only signs of grief. Had he really been this off base? Had he been listening to Laney too much? "Do you have paperwork to prove this?"

Sol raised his chin. "Of course. Would you like to see it?"

"If you wouldn't mind."

"I'll find the information you requested, but you're wasting valuable time." Sol's nostrils flared. "My Sarah is out there. Someone has her. And with every second that passes, I fear I'll never get her back."

"I assure you that we're working on it."

"Shouldn't you be questioning Laney? She should be behind bars now."

"You've got to believe us when we say we're doing our jobs," Jim said. "Now, that information? Please?"

Mark let out the breath he'd been holding as Sol disappeared upstairs. That had been uncomfortable. He was used to asking difficult questions in his role as detective, but turning the tables on a victim—making them feel like a bad guy—was one of the worst feelings ever.

Mark let out a long breath as he relived sneaking into Sol's house yesterday. It could have turned out badly. Very badly. He and Laney had escaped with new insight, but now he had to figure out the best way to use that intel without showing his hand.

Sol was acting suspicious, though. He couldn't deny the possibility that Sol was hiding something. Speaking in a foreign language, those driver's licenses, the drop-off that he didn't mention to the police...those things raised some red flags.

"I can understand why he wouldn't be forthcoming with this data. Especially if he didn't think it affected Sarah. He didn't want to risk it being leaked," Jim said, tapping his pen on the table. "Finding out you're adopted can shake up a person. My wife found out when she was ten that she was adopted as an infant. She went to counseling for two years for abandonment issues."

Mark flexed his jaw as he processed Jim's comment. "But that fact could be a major factor in this kidnapping. What if the birth mother is involved in all of this?"

"The birth mother wouldn't ask for a ransom."

"You never know what people will do. We've been surprised on many occasions. There are people who kill for love. People who steal in order to afford food. Others who think they're doing what's best for their child by abusing them. Deep inside, perpetrators are able to justify their actions, from the harmless to the devastating."

"I can't argue that."

Mark glanced at Jim, studying his partner's face. The man was smart. He'd been a cop for a decade longer than Mark, and he'd always trusted his opinion, even if he could be a hothead at times.

"Have you heard any updates on those men we shot yesterday?" Mark asked, remembering the invasion at Trent's house.

Jim shook his head. "We still haven't been able to locate them."

At that moment, Sol pounded back down the

stairs with papers in hand. He slapped them on the table. "There. Are you happy now?"

Mark picked up the document on top. It was a contract with an adoption agency. His name was there as well as Sarah's and it looked legitimate. Maybe this was another dead end. What if Jim was right? Had Laney planned this to buy more time? Was she just like his ex-fiancée—a master at manipulating things?

He mentally gave his head a little shake as he remembered the various attempts on her life. Maybe she was just as much a victim here as Sarah. There were a lot of facts and speculation that he needed to sift through.

"I'm sorry we bothered you with this, Mr. Novak," Mark said.

He scowled, as if Mark's apology meant nothing. "I insist that we keep this between us. When Sarah comes home, I don't want her to find out she was adopted. Not like this. She's already been through enough."

"I understand." Mark stood but paused before stepping toward the door. "Just a few more questions. Where did you move here from, Mr. Novak?"

His steely gaze met his. "Detroit."

"And are you thinking about moving again?"

He shrugged. "I'm not sure. I've thought about it. Why? Is that a crime?"

"Your daughter mentioned to her friend that you might be moving soon."

"My daughter can be nosy and overreact. That idea was simply thrown out as a possibility. Nothing was definite."

"And could you run through the scenarios with me one more time—about what happened yesterday when you left the envelope in the park? We're trying to identify the brunette who took the package you left."

His scowl deepened. "I've been through this multiple times already. I've already explained myself. These scumbags said if I got the police involved, Sarah would be killed. I wasn't willing to risk that. There was a jump drive inside with my bank information and pin numbers."

"I understand," Mark said.

Sol wasn't finished. "But you guys got involved anyway, and now you've probably ruined everything. These men—women—probably think I'm working with you. If Sarah dies, her death is on your hands."

Jim cut a glance at Mark and raised a hand, interceding between the two men. "We just don't want to miss anything. We realize this is stressful for you."

He glared and leaned closer. "You have no idea."

"We're not trying to cause you more distress," Jim continued.

"Well, you are. Now I could use some privacy. If you have questions about the drop I made yesterday, then refer to the notes I already gave the FBI."

Mark's thoughts felt heavy as they stepped outside. As they reached his sedan, Jim turned toward him.

"So what happened yesterday? We didn't have time to talk before you were shuttled off and hidden away."

Mark gave him a rundown on the events that had led up to Laney going into hiding. Maybe his partner would have some insight or see something Mark hadn't. This whole case grew bigger by the moment.

"So let me get this right. This chick—Laney, right?—she suddenly becomes proficient at shooting a gun?" Jim's eyebrows hung suspended.

"So she got a burst of adrenaline and wanted to defend herself. What's weird about that?"

"It just doesn't fit with what I know about her. I thought she was some kind of computer geek."

"She went to MIT. She's brilliant when it comes to technology."

Jim leveled his gaze. "She could have arranged all of this, you know."

"What do you mean?"

"If she's so smart, she could hack into whatever systems she wanted and change details to fit her story."

"If she was doing that, why wouldn't she conceal her text messages and email and bank accounts better?"

Jim shrugged, looking unconvinced. "You tell me. She's smart. Smart people can be conniving. You need to keep that in mind. It seems like the two of you are getting close."

"Don't be ridiculous. I'm just keeping an eye on her."

Jim gave him a knowing look. "Is that what they call it these days?"

Mark felt himself bristle. "That is all I'm doing."

"Well, the woman's nice to look at. I just don't want her to pull the wool over your eyes. I know a lot of good cops who've made bad decisions because of a woman.

"There's something I think you should see," Jim said.

"What's that?"

"Arnold—our new tech guy—was able to find some erased documents on Laney's computer. There were some email messages I think you'll find interesting." He handed Mark some papers.

"You printed them for me?"

"I thought they were that important."

Mark dragged his gaze away from Jim for long enough to scan the papers. What he read caused his spine to clench. This couldn't be right. It couldn't be.

They were messages dating back three months

ago between Laney and Nicholas, her boss. In the messages, every detail on what was happening now had been planned out, from the drugs to the licenses they'd hidden in Sol's house.

"What do you think now?" Jim asked.

"This can't be right."

"How else do you explain it?"

He shrugged. "Maybe someone set her up."

"Look at the time stamps. Arnold said they can't be faked."

"Anything can be faked."

Mark frowned, unwilling to believe any of this. But could he deny what was right before his eyes?

"I think Laney is putting ideas in your head. I urge you to be cautious, Mark. Someone's lying here. It could very well be Laney. You know how some women can be. Manipulators."

Yeah, Mark did know that. Visions of his ex-fiancée filled his thoughts. He'd let down his guard, let her into his life, and she'd betrayed him. She'd been trying to distract him all while her best friend was on trial for manslaughter, driving under the influence, and drug possession. She'd been waiting for Mark to mess up, to do something that the defense could use in court against him. Thankfully, he'd seen the light before anything had happened. Using him to get information.

Could Laney be doing the same? Preying on his kindness?

His gut clenched at the thought. He couldn't let that happen again. He'd gone as far as to voice his desire to take her out. What had he been thinking? He should have never said those words.

He was never, ever going to act on them, he promised himself. Never.

Laney paced the cabin as she waited for Mark to return. Devon and Eric, the two guards at the cabin, weren't talkative. They only stared at her when she asked her questions. At least they didn't try to stop her from doing her research on the computer.

Finally, after lunchtime, she heard a car pull up. She peered out the window and saw Mark approaching. She was practically beside herself as she rushed toward the door.

"You'll never believe what I found out," she told him as soon as he walked inside.

He pulled his coat off and hung it on a rack by the entryway. "What's that?"

She glanced at Devon and Eric before motioning for Mark to go into the dining room. It wasn't that she didn't trust the other two officers. But the less people who knew about this, the better.

"Look at this." She held up a picture of a little girl.

He squinted. "Who's this?"

"It's from Interpol," Laney said, talking too fast for her own good. Yet she couldn't seem to slow down. She had so much to share, and time was of the essence. "Fourteen years ago, a little two-year-old girl disappeared from Romania. She hasn't been seen since then."

Mark glanced up from the photo, a crease between his eyes. "And?"

She raised the photo higher. "There's no record of a certain someone's birth."

His lips parted slightly. "You think this is Sarah?"

Laney nodded, looking at the paper again, wondering why she didn't see this earlier. "Look at the similarities in their hair and eye color. This girl and Sarah are the same age. Plus, it happened in Romania. *Romania!* That could be the language that Sol was speaking—because that's where he's from."

Mark pressed his lips together a moment before shaking his head. "Laney, Sol admitted to me today that he adopted Sarah. Of course we're looking into it and want to confirm it with the agency. But it looks legit."

Laney's heart sank a moment as she questioned her own theory. It had made so much sense when she discovered the information earlier. But now she wondered if she was simply desperate for answers. Was she seeing things that weren't there? Was she drawing false conclusions in an effort to make sense of things?

No, she had to think this through. She was right. She had to be.

"What if Sol kidnapped Sarah when she was a child?" she finally said.

Mark stared at Laney, his eyes hard and unyielding. "Why would he do that, Laney? Would he be that desperate for a child? Maybe we're reading too much into this. Speaking a second language doesn't make someone guilty."

She couldn't let this drop. Not yet. "Then how do you explain those licenses that we found hidden in his house?"

He raised his hands and shrugged. "I can't. You didn't plant them there, did you?"

Outrage burst inside her until she started talking rapid-fire. "What sense would that make? It's not like I'm an expert in making fake licenses."

Mark leaned closer, not breaking his gaze. "I'm just trying to examine every angle, every possibility. There's a lot about this case that doesn't make sense."

"Do you think I hired someone to try to kill me also, so I would look like the victim?"

His expression sobered. "No, I don't."

"Then why are you being so stubborn?"

He didn't say anything.

Her shoulders slumped. Mark didn't believe her. He'd been the only one she thought was on her side. Without his support…who could she count on?

The answer felt stark and cold, yet clear. No one. There was no one she could trust. She'd known that from the beginning, though, hadn't she?

She raised her chin, unwilling to admit defeat. "I'm telling you that there's more to the story. Sol is connected with these kidnappers somehow."

Mark continued to stare at her. There was something different about him. What had happened in the short time he'd been gone? What lies had someone told him?

"Maybe that woman from the park—from the driver's license—was Sarah's birth mother," Mark said. "Did you consider that?"

Laney shook her head, trying to process that theory. "If that woman was Sarah's mom, then she'd run hard and fast after she grabbed Sarah. She wouldn't look back. She wouldn't ask for a ransom. She'd want to keep Sarah and hide somewhere and never be found."

He planted his feet in front of her, still unyielding. "I agree that there's more going on here than meets the eye. But I'm not willing to concede that Sol is involved in the disappearance of his own daughter. I have to keep an open mind here. Having tunnel vision has never helped solve any crimes."

What had happened to cause him to change his mind? When he'd left this morning, he'd been on her side. Yet somehow that had flipped and he seemed almost hostile now.

That's when she realized why. "It's your partner, isn't it? Jim? He changed your mind."

When Mark looked away, Laney knew she'd hit on the truth. "I have to be logical here, Laney. That's my job. Besides, if my past has taught me anything, it's to keep my eyes wide open."

She threw her hands in the air, her frustration rising until she couldn't contain it anymore. "You've seen everything that I've seen. You know those men tried to kill me. I'm not making that up."

"I agree that your life is in danger. I'm committed to protecting you."

"You're committed?" Something about his words caused outrage to shoot through her. They shouldn't. Mark had never promised her anything. He was a cop. That was it. Not a friend. Not an ally.

He was just doing his job.

Even if he'd said he wanted to get to know her better at the end of this, she could now clearly see that something was different. He must have had a change of heart.

Despite those realizations, frustration rose in her and she stood. "If you'll excuse me, I'm going to lie down for a while."

"Laney—"

She didn't bother to stop. She needed to be alone.

Just like she'd convinced herself she would be for the rest of her life.

SIXTEEN

Mark couldn't shake the cloud hanging over him. It was ridiculous and he knew that. Yet despite the fact he knew that he was being irrational, he felt unsettled at the idea of Laney being upset with him.

Had he betrayed her? No. Of course not. He was doing his job, and part of the requirement was to remain objective. To not get personally involved. To do everything legally within his power to find the truth.

But he knew there was more to it. He was beginning to care about Laney. To really care. To long for more than what their relationship was now.

And yet he'd just thrown her under the bus. Not for anything she'd done. It wasn't even Jim's influence, as he'd initially thought. No, this boiled down to Chrystal and her betrayal.

His heart pounded in his ears at the revelation. He had to make things right.

For so long he'd been focused on the loss of Lauren and his mom. He'd turned to law enforcement to make a difference, yet he'd been burned there too.

Lord, I can't hold on so tightly to the past, can I?

A verse from Micah floated through his head about what the Lord required of him. It said one should act justly and love mercy and walk humbly with your God.

Not everyone was the devil in sheep's clothing.

It was going to take justice, mercy and humility to put that into action.

Just then, his phone buzzed. It was the captain.

"Mark, any updates? Has Ms. Ryan shared anything of interest yet? Anything that will lead us to Sarah?"

Mark leaned against the wall, his inner turmoil tearing him apart. "No, sir. I'm still working on her."

"Jim told you about those emails we found on Ms. Ryan's computer."

Mark frowned as he remembered the conversation. "Yes, sir."

"I have a good mind to tell you to bring her in. But I'm still convinced that she could lead us to the girl. That's why I'm counting on you, Mark."

Mark shifted uncomfortably. "What about the FBI?"

His voice hardened. "They're doing their investigation and we're doing ours. We're working together wherever we can. Sol is about to go on TV and plead for these men to return his daughter. We'll see if that spurs anyone into action. We can only hope so. So you know what you're supposed to do?"

Unease sloshed in Mark's gut. "Watch her. Get her to trust me. Hope that she leads us to Sarah."

"That's right. Keep me updated."

"Yes, sir." But, even as he said the words, his heart felt heavy with betrayal and guilt.

With proverbial steam still coming from her ears, Laney hopped back onto the computer. How could Mark still question her? After everything he'd seen?

There was only one way she knew to cope with this situation, and that was to get online and do what she did best: research.

The men she'd once worked for had noticed that she put up a new firewall. With that in place, they wouldn't be able to operate. Wouldn't be able to put their scheme into action or access information they needed.

But that wasn't enough for her.

Spontaneously, she typed in Romania and terrorism into an online search engine. A few results came up, but one in particular stood out. Vechea Garda, which was Romanian for *Old Guard*.

She quickly began searching through all of the articles she could find on the terrorist organization.

She sucked in a breath when she came across data on the FBI's website. There, in one of the pictures, was a man named Vasile Dalca. If she took away some hair, added glasses and new clothing, he'd look just like... Sol Novak.

She sucked in a breath.

Sol *was* involved in this.

Would Mark ever believe her? Even if he saw this? Or were his blinders permanent?

She couldn't let herself get her hopes up. It was like she told herself before: the only person she could depend on was herself. She couldn't forget that, even if her heart begged otherwise.

How could she possibly track these men down, though? There had to be a way. Everyone left some kind of digital footprint.

What if she could set up a trap on the old firewall she'd created? If she could reinstate another firewall that looked similar? But when someone accessed it, it would lead to their location?

It was worth a try.

She emerged from her room and walked toward Mark's door. She'd do her best to convince him. He'd proven himself trustworthy in the past.

Before she had a chance to knock, his voice drifted from the other side.

"Watch her. Get her to trust me. Hope that she leads us to Sarah."

Laney pulled back as if she'd been slapped.

She was just a part of Mark's assignment. She'd known that at gut level. But she hadn't realized that all of his interactions with her had just been a ruse. He wanted her to open up to him, to trust him enough that she'd reveal where Sarah was— as if she knew.

Hurt flooded her heart. First she'd blindly believed Nicholas when he said he worked for the CIA. Now she'd believed that Mark might actually care about her when all he really wanted was to use her for information.

What had his boss directed him to do? She could hear the conversation now:

Act like you're falling for her.
Do whatever you have to do.
Break her heart if that's what it takes.

Was there anyone she could trust?

No, there wasn't. She'd known that all along. But for a moment she'd allowed herself to believe. To hope. To dream of the future.

That had all been a mistake.

She should have known better.

Mark pulled the door open and blanched when he saw Laney there. Had she overheard his conversation with Captain Hendricks?

Based on the pain flashing in her eyes, she had. He wished he could deal with this situation now, but he couldn't. He didn't have time to explain himself. He had to meet Jim and pick up something at a location twenty minutes away. The captain didn't want anyone—including Jim—to know Laney's whereabouts. Jim only knew she was tucked away for safety reasons.

"I have to run somewhere, but I'll be back in less than an hour," he told her.

She said nothing, only stared at him, a mixture of anger and hurt in her gaze.

His heart lurched. He longed to explain things. But then he remembered the evidence that continued to stack up against her. Until he was one hundred percent certain of her innocence, he had to keep his distance. He couldn't allow himself to be duped or to be distracted from this investigation.

"Of course," she finally said.

He paused again, his emotions and logic colliding with each other. Keep your distance, he reminded himself. *It's the smart thing to do. Getting attached will only lead to hurt and heartache.*

He skirted around her, refusing to give in to his compassion. He quickly explained to the other two officers that he had to run somewhere and then, with one last glance at Laney, he slipped outside.

He'd turned over thoughts of those deleted messages. It was true that they were dealing with some highly qualified hackers who could probably manipulate data like that. It was also true that someone was desperate to frame Laney.

So why had he questioned her innocence?

It was a mixture of exhaustion, stress and mistakes from his past he realized as he headed down the road. Jim had been convincing and all of the old feelings he'd felt toward Chrystal had resurfaced.

Was it really fair to pretend that Laney was Chrystal? He knew the answer. Of course not.

When he got back, he needed to somehow make things right.

Mark pulled up to the gas station where he was supposed to meet Jim. There were no other cars there, except a run-down Camaro parked by the back of the building. Jim definitely didn't drive that kind of car, and Mark would guess it belonged to the clerk inside.

So where was Jim and the evidence that Mark had to see with his own eyes?

He glanced at his watch. He'd actually arrived about five minutes later than scheduled. Jim was always on time.

Unease grew in his gut. He'd wait a few more minutes but then he was calling Captain Hendricks back. He preferred, since it was his job to watch over Laney, that he was actually there with her. It wasn't that the other two officers weren't competent. It was simply that he knew the intricacies of the case...the intricacies of Laney, for that matter.

As he waited, he continued to mentally review

the situation. The twists and turns it had taken continued to surprise him.

He knew one thing for sure: with every minute that passed and Sarah wasn't found, the chances of bringing her home alive diminished. They had to find her—and soon.

Finally, fifteen minutes past the time he was supposed to meet Jim, he called his partner. No one answered.

That was strange. Jim always answered, unless he was in the middle of an arrest or interrogation. But Jim was supposed to be meeting him now.

He hung up and tried Captain Hendricks, who answered on the first ring.

"What's going on?"

"Jim's not here," Mark muttered.

"He got caught up in an interrogation. The FBI was able to find the man who hit Ms. Ryan with his truck and then ran. They tracked down his image from some traffic cams. Jim convinced them to let him be involved in questioning the man. It all just happened in the last twenty minutes."

Mark bit back his irritation. The good news was the man might lead them to answers. The bad news was all this might be for nothing. What was so much of a secret that the captain couldn't just tell him over the phone?

"What about the evidence he needs to show me?"

"It's going to have to wait. Sorry."

Mark hung up and started back to the cabin. He hoped his feeling of impending doom was wrong. But it rarely was. Besides, this whole situation had proven to be a disaster left and right.

Laney had been pacing since Mark left, feeling beside herself with worry and agitation. How could she have been so stupid? She should have known better. But, as always, she too easily trusted. She believed the best in people when she shouldn't.

And now everything was a mess. Her heart included. As if she didn't have enough going wrong without letting her romantic feelings for Mark grow.

That did it. She had to do something useful. She grabbed her laundry into a big pile, explained to one of her guards that she was going to put a load in, and then she went downstairs to the basement.

She took her time loading the washer, pacing as water filled the basin.

The basement was fascinating with lots of closets and storage. She wondered who'd lived there before, how law enforcement had come to use the place, and who else they'd hidden there.

She paused by an abnormality on the wall. A breeze seemed to seep through the cracks in the paneling there. Interesting.

She felt along the section, looking for any kind

of evidence that her hunch was correct. She didn't see any kind of lever. She glanced at the floor. There was no sign that this was a door—no scrape marks or hinges or handles. But she was determined to do something to occupy her thoughts. This seemed just as good as anything else.

In a last-ditch effort, she placed her fingertips in the cracks and tugged. To her surprise, the wall moved.

Bingo!

She pulled the panel back and saw a wine closet on the other side. *Brilliant design*, she mused. There wasn't a speck of daylight to be seen in this room, and the darkness would help preserve the liquid.

As the water pouring into the washing machine stopped for a moment, another sound filled her ears.

What was that?

She froze, listening more closely.

Before she could ascertain what was going on, the machine kicked back on. She rushed toward it and turned it off, carefully closing the lid.

She'd heard something unusual. She just needed to figure out what.

As she glanced at the narrow window at the top of the wall, she quickly knew the answer.

Men were outside the cabin.

She didn't need to see them to know they were the bad guys. Somehow, they'd found her.

She started back upstairs to warn her guards when she heard the first gunshot.

The men were inside.

And they'd taken down her security detail.

Panic rushed through her. They were going to find her. And when they did they'd torture her until she did what they wanted.

She had to act. Now.

She rushed toward the wine cellar and pulled the door back, careful to be quiet. Then she slipped inside the dark space and carefully closed the door, concealing herself.

Her heart pounded in her ears. Would her plan work? She had no idea.

Dear Lord, please close the eyes of those pursuing me. Please keep me hidden.

As she muttered "amen," she heard movement. Someone was coming down the stairs, she realized.

She quickly turned her phone's light on and shone it around the room. Cobwebs hung in corners and shelves. Numerous bottles of wine rested in the spaces meant to cradle them. But that was it. There was nowhere to hide in this room. There was no escape if those men found her. She'd be cornered.

She closed her eyes and flipped off the flashlight app before pressing herself against the door. If only there was some kind of lock.

Wait—had she closed it all the way?

She ran her hand down the edge and it felt flat. Relief filled her.

Footsteps sounded right outside the door.

Her breath caught. The men hunting her were close.

Were they close enough to feel her terror? She knew the thought was ridiculous, but her terror felt palatable. She halfway feared her heartbeat was just as loud for them as it was in her own ears.

Calm down, Laney. Stay rational.

"Where is she?" a deep voice said on the other side of the door.

"Maybe she knew we were coming and ran."

"How would she have known?" Deep Voice said.

"Beats me. Maybe Detective James took her with him."

"That wasn't supposed to happen," Deep Voice growled. "Besides, if not that, then where did she go? She couldn't just disappear."

"We've searched every inch of this place, and she's not here. You tell me what happened."

The other man grunted. "Nikolae isn't going to be happy."

"What should we do?"

"Let's check this place out one more time. And then we'll have no choice but to tell Vasile what's going on."

Just then a shadow filled the crack of the doorway where she hid.

She held her breath.

Had they discovered her hideout?

SEVENTEEN

Mark hit the accelerator harder than necessary as he sped back toward the cabin. With every minute that passed, his certainty that something was wrong was only solidified. The pieces just weren't adding up.

It was almost as if he could feel trouble approaching like a deadly storm on the horizon. He couldn't get back to the cabin fast enough. When he pulled down the gravel lane leading toward the safe house, his gut clenched.

On the surface, everything appeared okay. There was no sign that anything bad had happened. No strange cars, mysterious men, broken windows.

But Mark still wasn't convinced.

As soon as he stepped from the car, he drew his gun. His gaze scanned the woods, looking for any signs of trouble.

He didn't see anyone.

He glanced down at the dirt comprising the

driveway. Footsteps were stamped there. Military-style boots.

None of his men wore that type of shoe.

His gut clenched tighter.

He considered calling for backup but changed his mind. The whole scenario that had just played out with Jim and the captain was part of what left him feeling unsettled. He'd almost felt like someone was trying to lure him out of the cabin. He hoped his gut was wrong. Prayed it was wrong, for that matter.

He hurried toward the front door and planted himself against the wall, listening for any telltale sounds inside.

Silence stretched around him.

Moving quickly, he pivoted toward the entryway and threw the door open.

Devon lay on the floor. Blood stained the area near his heart.

Mark's stomach dropped. No. Not Devon.

He leaned down and quickly checked for a pulse. Just as he feared, there was nothing there.

The ominous storm he felt approaching on the horizon grew darker, scarier and more imminent by the moment.

What had happened here while he was gone?

Remaining on the edge of the room, he checked each area of the first floor. It didn't look like much of a fight had ensued. Most likely his men had been ambushed. In a sneak attack. The bad guys must have appeared from nowhere and ended their lives with a quick pull of the trigger.

He reached the back door and found Eric dead, the same MO as Devon.

God rest their souls.

But where was Laney? Had the men grabbed her and run? He would check the upstairs and the basement first before calling the FBI. He needed to have all of his facts straight before taking any more action.

His shoulders felt heavy, like something unseen pressed on them with every step he took. None of this was supposed to happen. He was supposed to watch over Laney. And after their last conversation, she probably now thought that she was just a job to him and nothing more.

That couldn't be farther from the truth.

But would he ever have the chance to tell her that?

He hurried upstairs and checked under the beds and in the closet. It was clear.

Finally he went down to the basement. At his first step on the stairs, he heard a creak at the bottom. He instantly went on guard.

Was someone still there? Were they waiting to ambush him?

Cautiously, he lowered himself down toward the bottom, bracing himself with every step he took. He prayed he wouldn't find Laney like he'd found Devon or Eric. Prayed that she was okay. That somehow she was safe.

At the bottom of the stairs, he paused and scanned the area.

Nothing seemed out of place.

Except for a pile of clothes. Laney's clothes.

Had she come down there to do laundry? Had the men shown up when she did?

His throat tightened as an image of him finding Laney in a dark corner, also with a bullet hole through her chest, filled his thoughts.

Except that those men didn't want to kill her. They wanted—*needed*—her alive.

He turned sharply to the left by the stairway, making sure no one was waiting for him there. There was no one.

He opened the first door he came to—a closet of some kind. On the other side was a water heater and some cleaning supplies. No one. Nothing.

He wasn't sure if he was relieved or even more upset.

He went to the next closet. Inside there were only boxes.

He sighed. There was no one down there and nowhere else to hide.

Did that mean they'd taken Laney? How was he going to get her back?

Before he could formulate his next thought, he heard movement.

He drew his gun and prepared for the worst.

* * *

Laney saw the shadow pass over the slight, thin crack where the wine cellar door met the wall. Her heartbeat went into hyperdrive again.

Were the men back?

It had been silent for twenty minutes. She thought for sure the men had left, but she wanted to be careful, just in case they were waiting for her to emerge. She didn't want to hand them a victory, especially if she had any control over it.

She waited for several minutes while silence stretched again.

Maybe she'd been hearing things. Or maybe whoever it had been had left. Could she dare to hope? She couldn't stay there forever. Eventually she had to face the darkness on the other side of this wall.

She nudged the door open a crack, praying as she did so. Her muscles trembled and she could hardly breathe.

She peered through to the basement on the other side. In her limited line of vision, everything appeared okay. She didn't see any men hiding or strange shadows or signs of violence.

Drawing in a deep breath of courage, she shoved the door farther, trying to be as quiet as possible. Before stepping completely out, she took one more survey of the room and saw no one.

Maybe she had been hearing things.

Just to be safe, she grabbed one of the old wine bottles and held it like a club. It wouldn't be much protection against a bullet, but having something in her hands made her feel more prepared somehow. It was better than nothing.

She stepped out. As soon as she did, she sensed someone behind her.

She gasped and turned.

"Laney?" Mark. He stood there, waiting with his gun drawn. Ready to attack. To lunge. To fight.

Her muscles went weak so quickly that she dropped the bottle and it shattered on the floor. At once Mark gathered her in his arms.

"You're okay," he muttered.

"You're here." She could hardly believe her eyes.

"I thought for sure they'd gotten you." He cradled her head against his chest.

Laney could feel his heart pounding beneath her ear. He'd been worried. Even after everything that had happened. Even after revealing that she was just a job.

He'd still come back for her. That made her want to do cartwheels.

At once she remembered the reality of the situation. "How are the guys upstairs?" she asked.

He stepped back just far enough to look her

in the eye. Sorrow lined the depths of his gaze. "They…they didn't make it, Laney."

She shook her head. She'd known. Deep in her heart she'd known Devon and Eric hadn't made it. But she'd hoped for different results. She pressed the corners of her eyes as moisture pooled there.

"This is all my fault."

"Don't go there. You didn't pull the trigger." Mark wiped away a stray tear before pressing his lips into her forehead. When he stepped back, his eyes looked serious and grim. "We're going to have to talk later and get out of here now. Okay? I don't know where these guys went, but they could come back."

She pulled herself together for long enough to nod. "Okay."

As he led her up the stairs, a flutter of nerves rushed through her. What would she see up there? She didn't want to face it.

"Close your eyes," Mark instructed, almost as if he could read her thoughts. "You don't want to see this, Laney. You'll never forget. Ever."

The stark reality of his statement hit her. They were going to have to pass either Devon or Eric or both. Dead. It wasn't something she wanted to see.

"Mark, I need my purse and the computer in the bedroom," she said, trying to focus on their mission.

"Wait here and I'll get them for you."

"Thank you."

He hurried into her bedroom. She'd hidden both her phone and the computer in a safe in her closet. Mark had helped her find the hiding spot, so he knew exactly where they were located.

Laney kept her eyes on the wooden floor of the cabin. She was too scared to look anywhere else, too frightened at the possibility of what she might see. She already knew the horrors that had taken place there. The pictures she conjured up in her mind were enough to give her nightmares.

Enough to send her tumbling back in time to when she'd found... Nate.

Just as her mind started replaying that day, Mark appeared. "Let's go."

Thankfully he'd come when he had. She squeezed her eyes shut as he pulled her by the couch and table. She didn't open them again until she felt the gravel beneath her feet. As soon as she knew it was safe, she darted toward Mark's car.

Her heart pounded furiously as she climbed into the front seat. Without wasting any time, he took off down the road. It wasn't until five minutes into their trip that either of them spoke.

"I've got to call the FBI and let them know what's going on," Mark said.

"Of course."

There was so much she wanted to say to him. But was this the right moment?

Yes, she decided. She didn't know how much more time they had. This could very well be their last day. She didn't want to believe that. She wanted to hope that this situation was survivable. But she wasn't sure about that. These guys were determined to see them captured and eventually dead. Because that's how she would end up. They would torture her until they got what they wanted. But when all was said and done, she would be killed.

The thought gave her a dose of bravery. She had no time to waste.

Finally, Mark ended his call and turned to her. They were twenty minutes away from the cabin, closer to the mountains and farther from Richmond. He pulled off at an abandoned road and put the car in Park.

"I let the FBI know. They're going to go to the cabin with a team to investigate. I have orders to keep you safe and hidden."

His words caused a lump to form in her throat. "I understand."

He grabbed her hand. "I don't think you do."

"You're doing your job. I get that."

"It's more than that, Laney. Sure, it started as an assignment. *You* started as an assignment. But it's turned into so much more."

"What do you mean?" She had to ask for clarity. No more assumptions. Her heart couldn't handle them.

His eyes crinkled in thought. "You're all I can think about. I only want to be with you. I can't imagine never seeing you again when this case is done."

She could hardly swallow, hardly breathe. "Really?"

"Really. I'm sorry I didn't believe you. But I'm afraid people have been poisoning my thoughts. I should have never fallen for it."

"We've both believed things we shouldn't have."

His fingers brushed her cheek. "I'm sorry, Laney."

Her heart seemed to melt at his touch, his tenderness, his care. "I am too."

"I said this earlier and I meant it. When this is all over, I'd love to explore…us. I never thought I'd say that. That I'd want to give love a chance. But with you I do."

Her breath caught. "I feel the same way. You've made me feel things I haven't felt in a long time, Mark."

He gently brushed his lips against hers. The tension between them seemed to draw them together. Even when they pulled away, their foreheads still touched.

Her heart pounded in her ears as every sense

seemed to become alive and hypersensitive in his presence, at his touch, at his nearness.

"What now?" Laney asked.

Just as the words left her mouth, her cell phone rang.

She glanced at the screen, her eyes widening with disbelief as she looked back at Mark.

"It's Sarah," she whispered.

EIGHTEEN

"Sarah?" Laney whispered.

"Laney? Is that you? Is it really you?"

"It's me. Sarah, where are you?" Laney rushed as she put the phone on Speaker so Mark could hear.

"I'm at this old house near Staunton," she muttered. "I heard the guys talking about the town, but I don't know where we are exactly."

"Can you tell us about any landmarks?" Mark asked.

"Who...who are you?"

"He's a detective, Sarah," Laney said. "You can trust him."

"I...I don't know. There's an old barn out back. I'm in a house. I think it's three stories. It also has a basement. It's surrounded by nothing but woods."

Laney glanced at Mark. It wasn't a lot to go on.

"You're doing great. Is there anything else you can remember?" Laney asked.

"Oh—there's a river behind the house. A small one. A stream more like it."

At least it was something.

"Did you get away?" Laney asked.

"No, but the guys forgot to lock my door. I found my purse in the closet while I was looking for keys. I grabbed my phone and slid the battery back in so I could call."

"Is there anyone there with you?" Mark asked.

"Yes, there are a few guys here still. I heard them coming, so I went back to my room and closed the door. I figured if I had my phone, I had enough. I knew I could call you."

"We're going to find you, Sarah," Laney whispered.

"I hear someone coming. I've got to go, Laney. Please, come get me. Please! You're the only one who can help."

With those words, the line went dead.

Laney turned to Mark. "What do you think?"

"That's why she said your name when she called her dad right after she was abducted," Mark muttered. "We thought it was because the kidnapper looked like you—and she did. But I'd guess Sarah said your name because she was asking for you."

"What can we do?"

"I can call my contacts with the FBI."

Laney nodded. "While you do that, I'll see what I can figure out."

"What do you mean?" A knot formed between his eyebrows.

She opened the laptop, her mind racing. "I can pull up mapping programs that will show aerial views of the area. Maybe we can come up with a good guess, at least."

"It's worth a shot."

She narrowed her eyes at him. "I'm good at my job, Mark. I promise."

"I have no doubt. The breadth of what you're able to do just continues to amaze me."

Without wasting any more time, Laney accessed a satellite feed and narrowed the results around the small town of Crozet. The program she was using allowed her to apply a filter. She typed in stream and woods.

The results were still too numerous. She had no choice but to look at the town area by area until she found a place that fit the description Sarah had given them.

Failing wasn't an option right now.

Beside her, Mark talked on the phone to someone with the FBI. He started back down the road toward Staunton. They didn't have any time to waste.

Mark hung up. "Any luck?"

She shook her head, still staring at the screen. "Not yet. You?"

"The FBI is sending a team out this way. They also have a team at the office working on it.

They're trying to trace the call, but it was so brief that it will be difficult. It looks like the phone was turned off after she called because the GPS on it isn't working. Between everything, I pray we can find her."

"Me too." She stared harder at the map. She'd managed to find houses on small rivers with no barns, houses with barns but no river, and a house with a barn on a river but no woods.

Thankfully the area wasn't too large. Still, this would be tedious.

"We're about ten minutes away," Mark said. "Any idea of which direction I should head when we get there?"

"Not yet. But give me those ten minutes and I'll tell you." Urgency pressed on her even harder. What was she missing? The answers were there. She just had to look more carefully.

She paused at one area of the map and blinked.

Was that two houses beside each other? Or was one of the buildings a barn?

She zoomed in as close as she could, but the image was pixelated. She zoomed out again. The property had woods and a stream. There were two buildings, one was possibly a barn.

She hadn't found anything else and this seemed to be their best plan of action.

Then she remembered the tracker she'd placed on the server. In all the excitement, she'd forgotten about it.

She quickly logged on and checked the location tracker.

Bingo!

It had worked.

"I know where we need to go," she muttered. "I know where Sarah is."

Mark's fingers tightened on the steering wheel as they got closer and closer to the location where Sarah was being held. His mind turned over various scenarios, and none of them turned out well. Not with him going in on his own. He knew the FBI were still twenty minutes out, at least.

"You can't help me any more than you already have, Laney," Mark muttered, anticipating that she would want to assist him, but knowing that was a bad, bad idea.

He braced himself for her reaction. His muscles felt stiff and his mind couldn't slow down. The stakes here couldn't be higher—for Mark, for Laney, or for the country.

"I have to go." She crossed her arms and raised her chin in that stubborn manner Mark had seen many times. "I care about Sarah too, Mark. I want to help."

"It's dangerous for you to be there. If those men get their hands on you…"

"You'll be with me."

He shook his head, knowing this was no time to have a hero complex. "I'm not a superhero,

Laney. I can do my best to keep those men away, but I don't know what we're up against."

"I do."

He froze. "What do you mean?"

Laney proceeded to give him a rundown on the Old Guard. He'd heard of the organization before, but he never dreamt they could be involved now. Yet, at the same time, everything made sense. The accents. The motivation. The computer scheme.

Anxiety mounted between his shoulders. This could be even worse than he'd imagined. The terrorist organization had been known for random bombings. Apparently, they'd moved on to cyber terrorism, though.

He knew one thing: the members of the Old Guard would do anything to get what they wanted. Including murder.

"I need to keep you safe," he said.

"I'll never be safe, Mark. Not while they're out there. And I may be the only one who can stop them. I know how they think. I know how their computer systems work."

"What exactly do you think they're planning?"

"Best I can tell? They're going to hack into the US Treasury. They take our money. Watch our economy nose-dive. This country would never be the same."

"You think that's possible?"

"I know it's possible. Once the terrorists wreak havoc there, it will be the taxpayers who have to cover the damage. Records would be destroyed, accounts frozen, funds drained."

"You can stop them?"

"I already blocked their server. But if I can get into their computer, I can ensure they haven't taken any part of my work to use for their evil. That's what I fear they're preparing to do—to use my work to destroy good things."

The tension in his shoulders pulled tighter, stronger. "You're our most valuable asset right now. That's why you need to remain hidden."

She shifted in her seat to face him better. "Please. I want to go with you. I'll be smart. I promise."

"I have reservations about this. A lot." He had a feeling she wouldn't take no for an answer. And, once they got there, Laney was their best chance at accessing any computer information that might allow them to get past security systems and the like.

"I can do this," Laney pleaded.

He finally nodded. "Okay. You can help—but you have to let me call the shots. Agreed?"

"Agreed." She pointed toward a road in the distance. "Turn here. We're almost there."

Ten minutes later, they pulled off on a dirt road and concealed Mark's vehicle in the woods. They were going to have to go the rest of the way on foot in order to not announce their arrival.

Mark only prayed everything worked out.

* * *

Laney braced herself for whatever they might find. She knew this was risky. Really risky.

But it was worth the danger if it meant saving Sarah. Those men could do whatever they wanted to Laney—she wouldn't give them any of the information they were seeking. She'd give up her life if she had to.

"Are you sure you're okay?" Mark asked as they tromped through the woods.

Laney nodded. "Yeah. I'll be fine. One way or another."

He reached over and squeezed her hand, not letting go this time. "Losing you isn't an option, you know."

She craned her neck toward him. "It's not, is it?"

"I've lost too many people I care about, Laney."

Heat rushed to her cheeks. She cared about this man. She really did. Against all odds. Maybe even against common sense.

She touched his cheek, tracing his beard with her fingers. "I don't know how this will play out, Mark. But if anything goes wrong, it's because I insisted on being here. Always remember that."

Emotion flickered in his gaze. "Part of me wants to turn around right now and forget about all of this."

"We both know you can't do that. There's more on the line here than me and you and even Sarah."

He pressed his lips together, his expression looked grim.

Seeing him like that squeezed at Laney's heart.

But this wasn't the time to think about romance. There were other more important matters at hand.

He traveled through the forest until they reached the edge of the property. The sun was sinking low as they darted toward the side of the building.

Laney crouched down into the underbrush, careful to remain out of sight.

"Mark, someone is coming," she whispered.

They waited as a man and a woman came out of the back door and walked toward the woods. Smoke expelled from the woman's lips. They'd come outside for a cigarette.

"We're packing up and leaving tonight. It's just a matter of time before they find us," the man said.

Sol. Was that Sol? She cut a glance at Mark, and she sensed he was thinking the same thing.

"What will the police think when you disappear?" the woman with him asked. It was the brunette. The one whose hair was cut like Laney's. The one they'd seen at the park. She spoke with an accent, similar to the one she'd heard on the men in her hotel room.

Laney only hoped they didn't travel any farther than the property line. If they did, she and

Mark would certainly be discovered. The good news was that backup was on its way. But would they arrive in time?

"After the questioning I got today?" Sol took another long draw of his cigarette. "The police suspect I'm involved in this. At least that one detective does. He seems like the determined type."

"How did they discover you? We covered all of our tracks."

"We messed up that day at the park. From a distance, I wanted the police to think that it was Laney coming to pick up the money. But Laney was with the police. It was a close call."

"Smart thinking putting in the envelope the fake passport and license that I would need in order to escape the country," the brunette said. "At least I got that, in case we had to abort our mission prematurely."

Sol jammed his cigarette onto the railing surrounding the heating unit before dropping the butt on the ground and scowling. "Laney Ryan has nearly ruined our entire plan. We knew she was smart. She put things together much more quickly than I thought she would. That's why we should have killed her when we had the chance."

"She made the perfect scapegoat," the woman said. "She should be in jail right now, taking the fall for Sarah's disappearance. All the pieces were in place."

"But, it's like I just said, she was too smart. She

figured things out and fought harder than I gave her credit for. Now she put up a firewall, which has messed up our entire plan." Sol grumbled something beneath his breath.

"We need her to unlock it." The smell of smoke became stronger and Laney tensed.

Mark would be able to take down the two of them. But how many others were waiting at their beck and call? How would they get Sarah without the men hurting her?

"It's too late for all of that. We just need to get out of here before our entire plan is uncovered. Staying here puts everything on the line and we can't risk that."

"So we'll go back to Romania?" the woman asked, sounding sincerely surprised. "I was thinking an island in the north pacific maybe."

"We go back to our home country. With Sarah. We'll start a new life. We'll work from there. That's the nice part about the internet. We can do whatever we want wherever we want. We'll find another Laney who will help us."

"How will we do that?"

"We just have to do our research and know what the currency of our next victim is first," Sol said. "Laney's was easy—she wanted the luxury of being able to stay within the safety of her home. She wanted to pick up where her husband left off and protect the country."

Anger surged through her. They'd planned

out everything. Everything. They'd researched her past. Probably looked into her bank records. They knew what made her tick. How she operated. What was important to her.

And she'd been stupid enough to fall for it. She would never put herself in that position again.

"Of course, it helped that she no longer had a husband. The poor man died in the home invasion." Sol chuckled.

"A home invasion, huh?"

"That's what the police called it," Sol said.

Laney's entire body went tense. What were they saying? That... She couldn't make herself go there. She couldn't let herself believe it.

"What do you call it?" the woman asked.

"Collateral damage. Sometimes, to get the currency we need, we have to take matters into our own hands."

She let out a small gasp as a physical ache formed in her chest.

They'd killed Nate, she realized. Sol and his men had killed her husband and covered it up, making it look like a home invasion.

Tears pressed at her eyes. How could someone be so heartless? She'd always wondered if there was more to the murder than the police had been able to determine. But never had she imagined this...

Why hadn't she seen this earlier?

Her anger surged into rage. As she started to rise, Mark's hand came down on her shoulder.

"I'm sorry, Laney," he whispered.

Sol deserved to pay for what he'd done. The best way he could do that was at the hands of the justice system. It's what Nate would have told her. It was what Mark silently reminded her of now. She had to keep her cool here.

"All right," Sol said. "We pack up and need to be out of here in thirty. When daylight hits, I want this place to be clear. Then we put part two of our plan into action."

Laney wasn't going to let that happen…even if she died trying.

NINETEEN

As soon as Sol and his friend went back inside, Mark let out a sigh of relief. That had been close. Too close.

He and Laney stood, and he turned to face her. He could see the tears in her eyes and, without another thought, he pulled her into his arms.

"I'm so sorry." He said again as he rubbed her back, wishing he could take away her pain.

"They killed Nate," she said, her voice tinged with shock. Her body was stiff and each motion seemed stoic. "How could they be so cruel?"

"These men are willing to go to any lengths necessary to get what they want. I'm only sorry you've been one of their targets." They'd destroyed her life. He was determined not to let them destroy her.

Suddenly, she straightened and wiped her tears way. "We don't have time to wait for backup, Mark, or dwell on this. They're going to leave. We've got to move."

"We have no other choice. We can't take on everyone, Laney. They'll kill us."

"We've got to get Sarah before they take off with her. You heard Sol—thirty minutes."

"How do you propose we save her?"

She shook her head. "I don't know. But there's got to be a way." She glanced over at the house. "I think I know. Why didn't I think of this earlier?"

"What is it?"

"Sarah called me. What if she still has her phone and it's turned on now?"

"It's too risky to call her."

"No, but I can text her."

"What if the phone makes a noise to let her know?"

Laney shook her head. "It won't. She always has it on silent. Noises drive her dad crazy."

"We can try it. I just hope this doesn't backfire."

So did Laney. Her hands trembled as she typed, Where are you in the house?

She held her breath as she waited for a response. Finally, she saw that Sarah was typing something back!

Second-story bedroom facing the front yard. Are you here?

Laney typed back.

Yes, but we're waiting for backup. Do you know how many men are inside?

A moment later, Sarah typed: Six.

Laney leaned back, deep in thought.

"We know where she is, and we know how many men there are," Mark said. "There's still not a clear-cut way to get inside to rescue her without getting ourselves killed first."

"But you heard them. They're leaving in thirty. What if we lose their trail? If I may…I have another idea."

"By all means…"

"What if I set off the fire alarm inside the house?"

"How do you plan to do that?"

"I can use my computer to figure out what system they have. It won't be hard to make it go off. The men might think their cigarettes have started a small fire somewhere. It will distract them."

"What if they take Sarah and run?"

"It would get them out of the house, at least. Maybe we could take them down."

"At the sound of the first gunfire, they're going to be using Sarah as a shield."

"By the time all of this happens, backup will be here."

Mark let out a long sigh. "You really think you can hack into the fire alarm?"

She nodded. "I know I can."

"I suppose it's worth a shot. But, Laney..."

She started to pull her computer out. She paused as Mark leaned closer. Slowly, he pressed his lips to hers. Explosions sounded in her head and electricity traveled through her brain.

The kiss only lasted a moment when he pulled back and gazed at her.

"What was that for?" she asked, her lips still feeling like they were on fire.

"Just in case."

"In case what?"

"In case we don't get out of this alive."

Mark leaned over Laney, watching as she typed into the computer like a whiz. His eyes couldn't even keep up with how fast her fingers were moving.

A flowery scent tickled his senses. He wished they could relax. Maybe enjoy each other. But they couldn't. Not right now.

Not ever if they didn't survive this.

As they waited, he looked at the cars parked out front. Those men wouldn't get very far without any wheels.

Making a split-second decision, he pulled out his gun and put a silencer on the end.

"What are you doing?" Laney asked.

"Making sure these guys don't go anywhere." Aiming carefully, he hit each of the tires and watched as they flattened.

At least that was out of the way.

"How's it coming?" he asked Laney.

"I'm almost there. Just a couple more minutes."

As he waited, he pulled out his phone and called his FBI contact. No one answered. He looked at his screen and realized his signal wasn't strong there. Was that why there was no answer? Or was it something else?

"There," she whispered, closing the computer. "It's done."

Like clockwork, an alarm sounded in the distance. A moment later, men rushed from the house. Just as they suspected might happen, one of them dragged Sarah with him.

So far, their plan was playing out just as they'd guessed. But where were the FBI? They should be here by now.

"Did you see a fire?" Sol yelled.

"I didn't see anything," one of his men answered.

Just then, Sarah screamed. Mark's muscles tightened until he was ready to spring.

What was going on?

Before he could take action, he heard a stick break behind him. He turned in time to see three men surround them.

Laney bristled as the men stepped closer, guns drawn. Mark pushed her behind him as he faced the men.

"You're coming with us," one of them muttered. "Move!"

Having little choice, they walked toward the house. Sol was waiting there, a satisfied smile on his face.

As soon as they were close enough, he stepped toward them. She had no idea what was going to play out over the next several minutes, and she wasn't sure she wanted to find out. Anxiety tried to grip her, but she pushed it away.

"I was hoping I might see you again," he said, glaring at her. He quickly turned his gaze toward Mark. "I'm only sorry you're here to witness all of this. Thankfully, you'll be dead before you can report back to your superiors."

"Don't worry—they're on their way."

"Maybe they were. But a logging truck overturned and it's blocking the highway. Thankfully, Nikolae—Nicholas to you, Laney—was able to arrange that when he realized you were headed this way."

Laney's stomach sank. Was he bluffing? If he wasn't, none of them would ever see the light of day again.

They might let Mark go easily—with a shot to the head. They might keep Sarah, hoping she'll eventually see things their way. But Laney—they'd torture her until she did exactly what they wanted.

"You'll never get out of the US," Laney said.

"Then we'll have to implement our plan here and then die for our country."

"Why do you hate the US so much?" Laney said. "Why go through all of this trouble?"

"Would you believe me if I told you it goes back to the Cold War? Old ties with Russia? Loyalty toward people who fought to give us the life we have. The US doesn't deserve to thrive. We want people to know what it was like to stand in line for bread. To do without."

"That's a little extreme, isn't it?" Laney asked. "I mean, that happened decades ago. Sometimes you have to let things go in order to move past them."

"My family was killed during World War Two at the hands of American soldiers. So don't talk to me about being extreme. I want the US to feel the pain I did. To feel loss. To feel helpless to do anything about it." He offered a sardonic grin. "And for the money, of course." He raised his gun to Laney. "And you're going to help me make this happen. You think you're so smart and that you could stop us. But you can't."

"I'll never reinstall that program. Never."

Sol narrowed his eyes. "Never say never. Now move."

Laney flinched as he grabbed her arm and began pulling her toward the house. She dug her heels in, trying to stop him, to delay the inevitable.

A few minutes later, Sol shoved her into a room

and at a desk where a computer waited. "Reinstall it."

Laney shook her head with all the force she could muster to let them know how serious she was. She wasn't going to back down on this. "No, I won't do it."

Sol motioned to someone at the door, and Mark and Sarah were pushed inside.

"Work or I'll kill them."

Her heart jumped into her throat, nearly choking her with emotion. "No…"

An evil gleam hit Sol's eye. "You want to bet? I've worked my entire life to make this happen. Nothing and no one is going to stop me."

"I can't believe you'd sacrifice your daughter for this—even if she isn't really yours. You have been planning this from the beginning."

"For longer than you can imagine. Longer than you've been alive."

"I found out he kidnapped me when I was a girl!" Sarah shouted. "That's why he had his men grab me. I was going to go to the police with the information. He planned it so that other woman looked just like you, that way when I described her, you'd automatically look guilty."

He didn't deny it. "Don't worry, darling. You'll be safe. As long as Laney cooperates. I always knew you preferred her over me." The men aimed their guns at Laney.

"That's not true. I always thought of you as my father. I had no idea you were such a monster."

The smile dipped from Sol's face, and he dug the gun into Laney's back. "I've only ever loved you."

"Well, you sure have a funny way of showing it."

Laney had to buy time somehow until the FBI could get there. "How did you manage to lure Sarah into my house?"

"That woman was there," Sarah said. "I thought she was you at first, and I rushed inside, desperate to find out what was wrong. That's when someone jumped out and put a cloth over my mouth. I don't remember anything after that."

"I believe you, Sarah," Laney said.

"They wanted me to find my phone, Laney." Tears glistened in Sarah's eyes. "They wanted me to lure you here. I'm so sorry. I had no idea."

"I know," Laney said softly. "I know."

"Enough talk!" Sol shoved the gun harder. "Work! Now."

Laney began tinkering with the keyboard, her mind racing. How could she turn this to her advantage? She only knew of one option, and even that was risky. But maybe it would buy some time.

When Sol turned to talk to Sarah, she quickly pulled up a dummy website she'd been working on. It wouldn't fool him for long, but maybe for long enough that help could arrive.

Please, Lord.

"How's it coming, Ms. Ryan?" Sol growled.

"I'm doing everything I can," she muttered.

"Well, do it faster."

"You're not going to get away with this." She tapped more keys.

"Sure I am."

He'll kill us all when he's done with us. There wasn't a good way out of this. No matter how she looked at it.

Finally, she hit one more key and then pushed back from the desk. "There. It's done."

The gleam returned to Sol's eyes. "Great. Hayden! Come in here and check this out. Hayden is our computer expert," he explained with satisfaction.

She sucked in a breath. Hayden, if he was as expert as Sol claimed, would be able to identify what she'd done rather quickly. They were on borrowed time.

Her gaze shot to Mark.

He offered a slight nod to let her know he understood.

And, in one swift move, he kicked the gun from Sol's hand, and a shot fired through the air.

TWENTY

Mark lunged across the floor and grabbed Sol's gun. As he did, two men burst into the room.

Reacting swiftly, Laney grabbed Sarah and shoved her behind a chest of drawers, away from danger. For the time being, at least.

Sol wasn't going down without a fight. He drew his hand back and then swung at Mark. Mark ducked. He obviously needed to give the scrawny man more credit. That had been close.

As he straightened, a round of gunfire electrified the air in the room.

Mark dove onto the floor, near the desk. A bullet skimmed his biceps, but he ignored it and raised his own gun. He had to keep Laney and Sarah safe. He'd worry about his injuries later.

He began firing back at the men in front of him. Mark's first bullet hit the man he presumed to be Hayden on the shoulder, causing him to drop his weapon. He fired again, the bullet this time hitting the second man and taking him down.

Now it was just him and Sol.

Before Mark could stop him, Sol grabbed one of the guns his guys had dropped. He aimed it at Mark.

As he did, more footsteps pounded in the distance. Backup—for Sol—was on the way, which meant he'd be outnumbered again.

Come on, guys. Where are you?

Was the road really blocked because of an overturned logging truck? How long would that delay the feds?

He'd try for as long as he could to hold these men back. At least he could buy some time.

"Laney, the window," he yelled behind him, his gun aimed at Sol in a standoff.

He needed Laney to try and escape with Sarah. It was their best chance of surviving. Mark might not make it out of there, but at least the women could. That was all that mattered. Right now, he was in between the ladies and men who were after them. He needed to keep it that way.

"Don't move!" Sol shouted.

"You wouldn't shoot your own daughter," Mark said, praying his words were true.

"You have no idea what I'm capable of."

Mark kept himself between the ladies and Sol, stealing a quick glance back. Laney fiddled with the lock, trying to get the double-hung window open. Her hands trembled terribly. Finally, she nudged it upward.

"We can't leave without you," she shouted as men exploded into the room.

"Go! Get Sarah to safety."

"But…" She hesitated near the wall, crouching low, and holding Sarah's hand.

"No buts. Go. Now!" He fired his weapon, hoping he didn't run out of bullets. Because his gun was the only thing keeping him alive at the moment.

Casting one more glance his way, Laney finally nodded. She grabbed Sarah, and they climbed out of the window.

Now he had to figure out how he could escape there with his own life.

Laney ran through the woods as fast as she could, not looking back, just holding on to Sarah's hand. She had to get the girl to safety.

She didn't stop until she reached Mark's car. It was then she turned to Sarah. "I need you to wait here."

Sarah's eyes widened. "Wait here? Alone? Why?"

"I have to go back and help Mark."

"They'll kill you, Laney."

Her heart lurched. She didn't want to leave the girl. Didn't want Sarah to worry about her dying. But she couldn't leave Mark behind.

"I've got to do everything I can to help. You understand that…right? The FBI is on their way.

They should be here any time. But if something happens to Mark…"

Finally Sarah nodded. "Go. I'll be here. I'll be okay."

Laney stared at her another moment. "Are you sure?"

"Yes. I'll be fine."

With one more glance at her, Laney started back through the woods. Her mind raced. What would she do when she got there? How could she help? She didn't even have a gun.

It didn't matter. She had to at least try. That's what you did when you loved someone.

Loved…?

Did she love Mark? It was too soon, she realized. Certainly she couldn't love someone that quickly.

But she felt the beginnings of the emotion blooming in her heart. She hoped for more. That's why she had to do everything within her power to save him.

In the distance, she heard a car rumbling down the driveway. Her heart raced a moment.

Was it the FBI?

She hurried toward the edge of the tree line and saw a sedan pulling down the lane. She glanced at the driver.

I know him from somewhere!

After searching her thoughts for a moment, she realized it was Captain Hendricks. He'd made it!

Without wasting any more time, she flagged him down. He stopped the car and motioned for her to get in. She climbed into the front seat, feeling breathless with anticipation.

"What are you doing here?" the captain asked.

"You've got to help. They've got Mark inside."

"They've got Mark? He was supposed to wait for backup."

"We didn't have any time. We can explain all of that later. Right now, we just have to help him. Where is everyone else?"

"A log truck overturned. The road is still blocked. I managed to find another way around, though." He pulled over and put the car in Park. "We should go the rest of the way on foot."

She nodded, too shaken to argue.

He concealed the car off road and they started weaving through the trees.

"So tell me what happened," he said.

Laney gave him the rundown, her mind never leaving Mark for long. She couldn't help but picture him hurt. She only prayed that wasn't the case.

"The Old Guard is no one to be messed with," the captain said, sidestepping some underbrush in front of her.

As he said the words, tension pinched her spine. The Old Guard? She hadn't mentioned them. She'd only told Mark on their ride here, and he hadn't mentioned it to anyone, either. She'd heard all of his phone conversations.

The captain was working with Sol! It was the only explanation. No way had these guys been able to find all their locations so easily. They'd had an inside source the whole time.

Panic raced through her. What was she going to do?

She glanced around and finally spotted a thick branch.

She glanced at the captain again. He had a gun in his hands. But if she could take him by surprise...

Without wasting any more time, she grabbed the stick and swung it as hard as she could. It hit the back of his head, and he moaned before falling to the ground. His gun rolled out of his hand as he hit the dirt.

They both lunged for it at the same time, but Laney was quicker. She grabbed it and aimed it at him, her hands shaky.

"You won't do it," the captain mocked, sitting on a nearby rock and rubbing his head where she hit it.

"Don't test me, Captain," she seethed, the gun trembling in her hands.

"Maybe you should call me Nicholas."

The air left her lungs. "You are Nicholas?"

Satisfaction stretched across his gaze, his lips.

"That's right, Laney. It was so easy to pull the wool over your eyes."

"Why? Why would you do this?"

He shrugged. "This has been part of our plan for a long time. I came here as a young teenager, integrated into society, gained a position of power. It was all for this moment. All for a bigger purpose."

"I don't know how you can live with yourself."

He stood and stepped closer to her. "Quite easily. It will be even easier once I get the money that's rightfully mine."

"Stay where you are or I'll shoot."

Fire flashed in his gaze. "You'll go to jail."

"It will be worth it if it stops your plan from being accomplished."

"Nothing can stop us. You ensured that, didn't you? Thanks for your help."

"I'll do everything in my power to stop this. I can promise you that." Before she could question her decision, she fired.

The bullet hit the captain in the knee. He groaned and grasped his injured leg, all while muttering under his breath.

He wouldn't be going anywhere for a while. As a safety precaution, she grabbed his phone.

She took one last glance at him before continuing toward the house. She didn't have any time to lose.

She hurried toward the outside wall and pressed

herself there. Carefully, she scooted around toward the window where she'd escaped. She could hear voices coming from inside.

"What just happened?" Sol yelled.

"Beats me."

"Don't just stand there. Go find out!"

Laney peered into the window.

Her heart squeezed with pain. Mark sat in a chair, his hands tied behind him, while Sol paced in front of him. His lip was bloody, one eye swollen and a gash stretched across his cheek.

It was just a matter of time before these men killed him.

How was she ever going to rescue him?

She heard someone coming from the side of the house and ducked behind a shrub. She let out a sigh of relief after they'd passed.

Originally, there had been six men there. Mark had injured a couple during the earlier gunfire. How many more were left? Four?

There had to be something she could do. She studied the ceiling for a moment and saw the metal pipe running there.

Sprinklers.

She had an idea.

As soon as Sol paced away from the window, she aimed her gun toward the ceiling and hit the pipe. Water began raining down in the room. Any type of moisture would ruin their computer equipment.

As the men scrambled toward the desk, Mark

managed to jerk his hands free from the binds holding them together. He swung the chair he'd been tied to and knocked out two men, taking a third one in a domino effect.

"Laney, go!" Mark yelled.

She wasn't going anywhere.

Laney fired at another one of Sol's men, and he went down. Mark brought the gun down on another man's head, knocking him out before he could do any more damage.

All the men were taken care of, except Sol. As Mark turned toward him, the man raised his hands in surrender. Mark pulled out some cuffs and put them around the man's wrists.

"Good job, Laney," Mark told her.

Just then, she heard cars behind her.

She glanced back.

The FBI was here. And all of this was over.

It was finally over.

EPILOGUE

It had been six months since the whole incident with Sol. *Six months.*

In some ways, it felt like a lifetime ago, Laney mused.

She was so glad that part of her life was behind her. She was now working and using her skills for the local police department in their forensic technology department. That meant she got to see Mark every day.

Truthfully, she was able to see Mark every day anyway. Soon she'd see him every night, as well.

In a few hours, they were getting married.

And Sarah would be at their side. Laney was in the process of officially adopting the girl, and she couldn't be more thrilled. Neither could Mark.

"Are you ready?" Tessa knocked at the door where Laney was getting ready before slipping inside. The two had become good friends after the incident with Sol.

Laney smiled, unable to resist patting Tessa's

growing stomach. She was due in four months. "I am, Mama. Thank you for standing up with me today."

"I'm thrilled to do so. Trent was just saying the other day that he's never seen Mark so happy. The old gang is out there—Trent, Mark and their friend Zach from the police academy."

"I'm glad they could all get together."

Tessa studied her again. "Mark is going to be blown away when he sees you. You look gorgeous."

Laney felt herself blush. "Thank you."

Tessa looped her arms through Laney's. "Come on. Let's get you out there."

Laney nodded, knowing without a doubt that this was the best decision she could make. There was no one else she'd rather be with than Mark—now and forever. Since he'd come into her life, things had changed—for the better.

She never thought she'd find someone who'd come close to holding a candle to Nate, but she'd found Mark. Both men were remarkable, and for that she was forever grateful. But Nate was in the past. She'd always remember him. Always love him. But now she couldn't imagine her life without Mark.

The two had decided to have a small ceremony—only a handful of their closest friends. It was taking place at Mark's church, which had recently become Laney's church. She'd even gotten involved in bible study there and had made a few friends. It was a start. With Mark by her side, she felt like she could do anything.

Sarah waited for her outside the sanctuary doors. She wore a lovely burgundy dress that came down below her knees. Her hair had been pulled into a twist, and a lovely diamond necklace that had been Laney's grandmother's hung around her neck. One of the few personal valuables she still possessed because, thankfully, she'd kept it in a safe-deposit box at the bank, along with her passport.

"Laney, you're gorgeous." She pulled her into a hug and lingered.

"Thank you. You look wonderful also." Laney's heart filled with gratitude that she had Sarah in her life.

The two had always had a bond. Now she'd be able to ensure that Sarah had the kind of teen years she deserved—one away from her controlling "father." Sol, for that matter, was now in jail and he'd be there a long time for the attempted cyber terrorist attack he'd almost set forth on the country.

He and his men had all had fake driver's licenses ready so they could escape in the aftermath. They'd been so close to making it happen. Even Captain Hendricks—Nikolae—had been found guilty on all charges. He would be spending the rest of his life in jail.

Sarah, in the meantime, had researched her birth parents, but they'd both passed away in a car accident four years ago. The news was tragic but it had made the adoption easier. One day they'd go to Romania and see where she was born. But one step at a time.

Sarah smoothed out the skirt of her dress and beamed under the compliment. She'd brought Danny with her as a date to the wedding, and she seemed truly happy, despite everything. It took a strong woman to get through what she'd been through. Both she and Laney would heal together.

"Thank you," Sarah said. "I feel like a princess."

Laney squeezed the girl's arm, knowing the music was playing and that it was time for the ceremony to begin. But there was something she had to say first. "Sarah, I'm really sorry about everything that's happened. But I'm so glad that you're going to be a part of my family. You're an answer to a prayer."

Tears welled in Sarah's eyes, but she quickly brushed them away. "I'm sorry about the way things happened too. But I would have never gotten through all of this without you. You're truly a lifesaver. God sent me to you, knowing I'd need you during this time."

"My thoughts exactly." Laney looped her arm through Sarah's. "You ready?"

Sarah grinned. "Let's do this."

Sarah gave Laney one last hug before gripping her flowers and starting down the aisle. She was the only bridesmaid that Laney wanted.

Finally, the doors to the sanctuary opened wide, and Laney made her grand entrance.

Mark stood at the end of the aisle, a huge grin on his face. The walk toward him seemed like both the longest of her life and like she floated all too quickly to the end.

Thankfully everything had worked out. Sol and his minions were now behind bars. The US financial economy seemed steady and unaffected by Vechea Garda's plan. Sarah had gotten through all of this amazingly well, all things considered. She'd have counseling for probably many years, and soon she'd like to go back to Romania to meet her biological father's family. Laney would go with her—and so would Mark. But she needed more time first.

"You look beautiful," Mark whispered as a soloist sang about a love to last a lifetime.

"Thank you." She squeezed his hands, the whole ceremony feeling surreal.

When the song ended and, as Laney went through her vows, she couldn't help but think how blessed she was to be able to find two good men in her lifetime.

Thank you, Jesus.

Finally, they said, "I do."

"You may kiss the bride," the minister said.

Mark leaned toward her and their lips brushed. When they pulled away from each other, both had huge grins on their faces.

"I now introduce you to Mr. and Mrs. Mark James!"

Everyone cheered as the pianist played the recessional.

Though they had a small reception planned at the church afterward, Laney wanted to grab a moment alone with Mark first. As soon as they reached the end of the aisle, she pulled him into one of the classrooms.

He raised his eyebrows mischievously. "I can't wait for a moment alone with you, either."

She giggled before turning serious. "I just want to let you know that I'm so thankful for you."

"I am too." He leaned his forehead against hers. "Suddenly, everything seems right. All that pain from the past…it's still there. But I finally feel like I can move beyond it."

She ran her finger across his cheek. "Me too, Mark. Me too. I feel like there's nothing the future can hand us that we can't handle together."

"After everything we've been through, I'd say that's true."

"I love you," she whispered.

His lips met hers. "I love you too. Always and forever."

* * * * *

If you enjoyed this story full of suspense and romantic tension, pick up these other stories from Christy Barritt:

KEEPING GUARD
THE LAST TARGET
RACE AGAINST TIME
RICOCHET
KEY WITNESS
LIFELINE
HIGH-STAKES HOLIDAY REUNION
DESPERATE MEASURES
HIDDEN AGENDA
MOUNTAIN HIDEAWAY
DARK HARBOR

Available now from Love Inspired Suspense!

Find more great reads at
www.LoveInspired.com

Dear Reader,

I've always loved spy stories. I think because they're so out of the realm of my ordinary life that they seem a bit like a thrilling roller-coaster ride—full of high-stakes adventure yet safe. The more dangerous, the better. Bring on the excitement—as long as I can stay safe in my little suburban house!

I've gone through the Citizens FBI Academy, as well as my local Citizen's Police Academy. People have asked me if I'd ever want to go into law enforcement. My answer is always a quick no—I'd be terrible doing those jobs!

I hope you enjoyed getting to know Laney and Mark. Their stories certainly intrigued me and kept me guessing as I wrote. Laney was falsely accused and was desperate to both clear her name and to rescue her neighbor.

Have you ever been falsely accused? Maybe your situation isn't anything like Laney's, but it's not fun when people make assumptions about you. I'm comforted by the fact that God loves me and sees me as I am.

I'd like to give a special thank-you to those who serve our country. From police officers to

firefighters, to the military and even the CIA—
you're doing a job I could never do. For that,
I tip my hat.

Many blessings,